Their

Christmas

Love

Silver Fox Christmas Book 3

Katie O'Connor

Snarky Heart Press

Their Christmas Love

Silver Fox Christmas Book 3

Katie O'Connor

Snarky Heart Press

−Their Christmas Love−
−Silver Fox Christmas Book 3−

This book is a work of fiction. Names, characters, places, and incidents are either products of the author's imagination or used fictitiously. Any resemblance to actual events, locales, or persons, living or dead, is entirely coincidental.

Published December 2022
(katieohwrites.com)

ISBN: Kindle Edition 978-1-989816-66-0
ISBN: Print Edition 978-1-989816-65-3
ISBN: Other Digital Versions 978-1-989816-67-7

Design and cover art by Laura Heritage P.S. Cover Designs
Editing by Samantha Talarico

Dedication

This one is for Dave and Linda.
Because one night, while drinking,
you told me to write a silver fox novella collection.
I am still mad at you both.

Their Christmas Love

Welcome to Christmas in Valley Springs the place that proves that the heart can still find love as you get older. Valley Springs is the home of the hottest silver foxes in Canada. Pop in for a while, read these heart-touching holiday romances featuring ladies and gentlemen in their fifties.

♥♥♥

Nora Ravine's been around the relationship block before and has a thirteen-year-old daughter to prove it. She's looking for long term and not just a fling because she has a heart and a daughter to protect. When NASA scientist Ross Roxx wanders into her orbit, she thinks he might be the one.

Ross Foxx isn't ready to retire. He adores Florida, and loves deep dives into math problems. Nora Ravine is a temptation he's having trouble resisting, but she won't follow him to warmer climates and he isn't ready to move to the frozen north.

Is the spirit of Christmas, and the joy of forgiveness, enough to carry them into a future together and help them find their Christmas love, or will they drift apart like snowflakes in a blizzard?

Chapter One

Ross Foxx stood at the end of his brother's driveway, staring at the trio of ladies as they walked away. It was only seconds until the snowfall obscured his view. Wow. Who knew that coming to Valley Springs for a visit would mean finally meeting a woman who made his heart pound? Nora Ravine was the loveliest woman he'd ever met, and he'd only spent five minutes talking to her.

She might be only five foot six, quite small compared to his six foot two, but holy Christmas, she was anything but ordinary. She had curves upon curves, even in her winter jacket. He'd almost been tongue tied trying to talk to her.

He was a mathematician for NASA for Pete's sake. He would talk to anybody. Literally anyone. He had talked to the President of the United States, the Queen of England, and the Prime Minister of Canada without issue. It had been years since a woman had left him tongue tied;

not since he'd met his wife, God rest her soul. He'd always miss Martha, but she'd been gone for decades.

Their kids were grown, and he was more than ready to start fresh. In truth, he'd been seriously looking for someone to love since the kids had left home for the Canadian military's train and learn program. Now, they were in their early thirties and well established in their careers. Rick was a doctor, and Todd a dentist. They were doing all right. At fifty-four, he was close to retirement age, but not certain he was ready.

"Holy cow!" His brother Tom's voice interrupted Ross's thoughts. "Declan, why didn't you tell us your lovely librarian had friends? Beautiful friends."

Declan and Thomas were his adopted brothers. They'd been together since childhood and were as close as blood siblings. He was in Valley Springs to visit them for a few days.

"Hey, I can't help it. I didn't know. And I certainly didn't realize that one of them was a famous sculptor. Eve Farstaad, who knew?" Declan shrugged and turned his attention back to the truck he was fixing. "I need to finish this so we can go inside, out of the cold. I'm chilled through."

"I'd rather go with them," Ross declared, nodding in the direction the ladies had taken, wishing he could have gone with them.

"You can't chase a woman here; you live in Florida."

"Hey, I can travel. I've got enough seniority that I can pick my vacation days. I can be back in Canada anytime I want. I'm here now, aren't I?" For a woman as lovely as Nora Ravine, he'd travel a long way.

He's been startled when she walked up to him and started a conversation. She was outgoing and interesting. He wondered a bit about the tiny spots of paint on her snug jeans, but it didn't matter. Paint he could live with. He would have loved to talk longer, but she'd said something about being behind schedule on a commission and ended the conversation.

"We should have asked them in for coffee," Ross said.

"I'm meeting Eve for drinks tomorrow. You should join us," Tom said. "I'll get her to bring her friends.

You should come too, Dec." He stuffed his hands in his pockets and blinked snowflakes from his eyelashes. The weather was turning nasty, and it was only October.

"Cool, I'm meeting Nora for drinks tomorrow too."

"We're going to the Ram's Head Pub."

Ross laughed. "We are too."

"I'll be staying home," Declan said sadly.

He was shy. He'd been burned by a woman when he was young and had never gotten over it. As much as he was interested in the local librarian, it would be almost impossible for Declan to ask her out. Ross felt terrible for his brother's terminal shyness.

"Hey, come with us. We'll get her friends to ask library girl to the pub. We can all have drinks. It'll be a party and that'll take the pressure off you."

"Her name is Cynthia. I don't know…" He paused. "I'm not sure it's a good idea." He wiped some grease off his tools and carried them back to his enormous toolbox in the spotless garage. He placed each tool in its proper spot with a mathematical precision that impressed Ross.

"I know I'm excited," Tom declared. "I can't wait to get to know Eve better. I can't believe I actually met the famous Eve Farstaad. I've admired her work for years. I'm hoping I can get a private viewing."

Ross laughed. "I'll bet," he said, waggling his eyebrows. "What part of her privates are you hoping to see?" Tom punched him in the arm. "Ouch. Dang it. What was that for?" He swatted Tom back.

"For thinking nasty thoughts about Eve," Tom growled. Declan and Ross laughed.

"Look at our baby brother," Ross teased, "all tied up in knots over a woman."

"What about you?" Tom snapped. "You were practically drooling on their feet. Disgusting."

"I was not drooling." At least Ross didn't think he was drooling. What if he'd made a fool of himself? That would suck. Wait, she'd agreed to go for a drink with him. That was the nice thing about a town as small as Valley Springs; you could ask a woman on a date, and she didn't run screaming, or need her friends along for protection. It sure wasn't like that in his Florida neighborhood.

5

"I don't know about you guys, but I'm starved. While you finish fixing the truck, I'll go inside and make something to eat." Ross turned to go inside.

"You're just going inside to fantasize about Nora," Declan teased.

"I'm not buying into your teasing," Ross said. "No way am I getting into an argument about this. We're adults now, we don't need to spend every waking moment razzing each other." Life as one of the Foxx brothers had always included a lot of teasing and wrestling. As adults, precious little had changed. They still pestered mercilessly, but with a lot of love in the background. At fifty-four, he was thankful their wrestling was a thing of the past. He wasn't up for that type of playful physical altercation anymore.

He left his brothers on the driveway and entered their kitchen. Declan had moved to Valley Springs; Tom had come along to help build Dec's house and ended up staying. Ross only came for visits. He adored his job. He could retire anytime he wanted to, but so far, he hadn't really felt the urge. He wanted something to do in his retirement, and he wanted someone to spend his money with. He was paid ridiculously well for what he did. It would be a shame for that money to sit in the bank forever. He didn't want to waste his money, but find fun and useful ways to spend it.

He loved his two sons, but had no urge to leave them a small fortune. He'd worked hard and wanted to enjoy the reward. Neither of his brothers were interested in travelling with him, not that he could blame them. He wanted a companion, a woman to share his life with. So far, he wasn't finding anyone in Florida, and the odds said he wasn't going to. Meeting Nora was a miracle.

Their Christmas Love

Chapter Two

Twenty-four hours later, Nora turned to her best friends and roommates, Cynthia and Eve. "I can't believe I'm going on a date with a virtual stranger. Am I nuts?"

"How is it nuts? You met a man and hit it off. The fact that you met him on the street is irrelevant," Cyn teased. "Seriously, this is Valley Springs. You're meeting him at the pub; what could possibly go wrong?"

"Cyn and I will be there too," Eve added. "I can't believe she's not travelling with us though. Declan is picking her up."

Nora squished in between her friends so she could see to comb her hair in the enormous bathroom mirror. "I really should renovate this bathroom; it's so eighties."

"The house was built in the eighties," Cyn replied dryly.

"Truth," Eve agreed. "If you changed out this big, old plain mirror, we couldn't get together for date preparation."

9

Nora laughed. "Honey, I'm hoping you'll meet someone and move out of my house." She was teasing and knew her friends would take it that way. She was happy to live next door to her ex-husband and daughter, and to share her four-bedroom house with her two best friends. "Ugh, I can't get the paint out of my hair."

"You're a wild woman with a paintbrush," Cyn responded. "You really should calm down."

"I was calm; I was finishing up a landscape commission, and I bent over and my hair swung forward and swiped the painting. I can't get it out. And I'm not going to use paint thinner on my hair."

"Definitely not," Cyn agreed. "It would totally destroy that lovely blonde color."

Nora pivoted to get a view of herself in the mirror. "I should diet. He's not going to like all these curves." She'd never been thin and had a hate-hate relationship with working out. She jogged on occasion and took a weekly yoga class, but working out was never going to be something she enjoyed. Combined with her love of food, she was a few pounds overweight. Not huge, but not thin either.

"Don't be ridiculous," Eve said. "You're perfect just the way you are. Curves are beautiful, and you're not even close to fat. Besides, he did ask you out, right?"

"I suppose. But—" She needed to get over this insecurity.

"No buts," Cyn said. "Just because your ex traded you in for a younger, thinner model, it doesn't mean you're not perfect the way you are. He's the tool."

"He's not a tool," Nora defended her ex who lived next door with his new wife. "We just…never mind." It wasn't worth discussing. She'd married too young, and they'd grown apart. They had a congenial relationship, and it was great living close enough to her ex that she could see her daughter, Melissa, regularly.

"The point is," Cyn said, "you're beautiful and curvy, and if what's his name wasn't interested, he wouldn't be meeting you for drinks."

"Ross, his name is Ross." She shook her head. "He's a mathematician. What can an artist and a math geek possibly have in common? This is doomed before it even starts."

"Don't be silly," Cyn admonished. "Creatives and logical people can make great matches."

"Besides, he's cute. All three of them are cute," Eve pointed out. "Maybe it'll just lead to some hot sack time. I'd be game for that."

Her laugh was infectious, and Nora joined in. "I think I'm more interested in conversation at this point." She paused dramatically. "But I'm not ruling hot monkey sex out entirely." She pivoted to look at herself again. Her dress was neither loose nor tight. The dark gray, nearly black knit fabric had a subtle red floral pattern. It came to just below her knee, right to the place her low-heeled boots ended. It had long flowy sleeves and a high scoop neck. It hinted at more than it showed. Most importantly, she felt feminine and pretty in it. "Do you think this dress is okay?"

"Okay," Cyn replied. "It's amazing. I told you it looked great when you bought it. You're going to wow Ross off his feet."

Satisfied that she looked acceptable, except for the paint remnants in her hair, she strode out of the bathroom. "Come on, Eve, let's do this. Catch you there, Cyn."

The pub was hopping. Friday nights usually were. Nora paused just inside the door and peered around. "They're here already." She pointed. "In the corner." She swallowed a lump of nerves and walked to the table, Eve right behind her.

"Hi." She smiled her warmest smile. Gosh, Ross was so handsome. Tall with dark hair, just starting to gray at the temples. Striking blue eyes. Totally drool-worthy and nothing like her ex. And those dark-framed Clark Kent glasses...she nearly swooned. When he noticed her, his smile lit the room.

Ross leaped to his feet and pulled out the chair next to him. "Here you go."

How old fashioned and sweet. She sat down, and he helped her pull the chair in. "You know, I don't need help to sit." She wasn't upset, just surprised.

"Of course not. I can't help myself. My mother taught me to be chivalrous. She'd be appalled if I didn't pull out your chair."

"Well then, thank you. How are you tonight?" A man who respected his mother was a good thing, right? At least as long as he wasn't a total mommy's boy.

"I am fabulous. The odds of me being any better, now that you're here, are astronomically small. Practically infinitesimal." He chuckled.

"Quit with the math talk," Tom said as he helped Eve into her chair.

"What can I get you to drink?" Ross asked.

"Oh, I'm not sure. Maybe a beer? No, wait, white wine."

He smiled, then gave a waitress a brisk nod. The twenty-something server hurried over, a huge grin on her face. "What can I getcha?"

"The lady will have a white wine; I'll have another whiskey, please." As the server walked away, he turned back. "Oh, I didn't ask, did you want something to eat? I'm weighing the options of a burger or a steak sandwich."

"A burger might be nice. I'll order when she comes back." His smile was breathtaking. Just being near him, smelling his cedar and musk cologne, was firing up all her nerve endings. Something about him had her on edge, in a good way. When was the last time she'd been this attracted to someone, this aroused, just by their proximity? Never. That's when. She'd never felt like this.

14

"Tell me about your art," Ross said.

"Oh. Yeah. Um." *Good grief, would aliens just swoop in and take her away?* She could hardly form a coherent thought, let alone a sentence. "I'm a painter."

"I love your landscapes. They're breathtaking, especially the ones with wildlife. It's almost as if the animals are going to step out of the painting. They're incredibly realistic."

"You know my work?" She was astounded and flattered.

"Honestly, I'd heard of Eve, but not you. Once you told me your name and that you painted, I looked you up. I hope that's not too creepy." He raised one eyebrow in question.

Was it creepy? Not really. She was, in a small sense, famous in the art world. She wasn't Group of Seven material, but she did okay. Someday, she'd like to be as famous as Emily Carr, but for now, she was content to earn a living. "It's okay. I get that a lot."

"I couldn't find a gallery showing your work."

The comment seemed idle, but held a wealth of questions. "I'm not showing right now. My contracts all

15

ran out and I haven't renewed them. I'm working on commissions. They're not my favorite, but they keep me busy while I build up stock."

"Don't you want to be in a gallery? I thought all artists dreamed of being shown. I know that Tom does."

"Tom's an artist?" She didn't know that. Of course, how could she; they'd just met.

"He's a master craftsman. He works in wood. Sculptures, furniture, toys, and trinkets. He says the wood tells him what to make." He shrugged. "I don't get it. Honestly, I don't understand artists. Math and astrophysics, yes; art, no."

She laughed. "Nobody does. Unless you've been bitten by the creative bug, you can't get inside the creative mind. My ex doesn't understand me at all. Our differences are probably part of the reason why we split up. He didn't understand how I could lose track of time when I was in my studio."

"Losing time when you're caught up in work is something I can appreciate. Give me a complex equation to solve and I'm gone until I figure it out." He chuckled. "You said ex; you're separated then?"

"Yes. Divorced actually. I live next door to my ex. We share custody of our thirteen-year-old daughter."

"Is that awkward?"

"Actually, not at all. It works out great. I have a very congenial relationship with him and his new wife. He moved here for work. Since I'm an artist, I can work anywhere. I followed him. I wanted to stay close to Melissa, to keep things stable for her." The awkwardness of their conversation was making her head ache. "How about you?"

"I have twin sons, they're thirty-four. Their mother died of complications after their birth. Raising two boys was tough, but they're doing well now. They actually graduated high-school at fourteen. They're kind of prodigies." Pride rang in his voice.

"Do they get that from you?"

"Actually, no. Their mother was brilliant. Smartest woman I ever met. She was a theoretical physicist and spoke eighteen languages fluently. She makes me look like a dunce. They got it all from her."

Wow. How was she supposed to stack up to that?
"You must miss her." Great, spout lame platitudes.

17

"Yes and no. I loved her, and I'll never forget her, but thirty-four years is a long time. I'm over her, at least as much as one ever gets over the loss of someone they love. Now, I think I miss the company, rather than the person. I'm past the major grief of losing her, but she'll always hold a small piece of my heart."

Aw. He was so sweet. Sweet, kind, and smart. So smart. How was she supposed to keep up, and where was the server with that wine? She was dying of thirst. She needed to wash down the lump of anxiety clogging her throat. She struggled for something to say.

"I'm sorry for your loss." She gave herself a mental eye roll. She was floundering here. She was outgoing. She could talk to anyone, but she was struggling to keep the conversation going. It was like when she was at a gallery opening and a guest didn't know she was the artist and told her how much they found her work simplistic or pretentious or just unattractive. Awkward.

"Thank you. It was a long time ago. I loved her, but I'm more than ready to begin a new relationship. That's why I asked you out."

"I'm glad you did." Okay, this was better. "How can you work for NASA and live in Valley Springs?" There were so many things she wanted to know about him. Did he love action movies like she did? What was his favorite food? How well did he kiss? She slapped duct tape on the thought and bundled it away. It was far too early to be thinking about kissing him. They'd just met.

"I'm not from Valley Springs. Dec and Tom live here. You've been past their house. I live in Florida. I'm just here visiting."

"Oh." Why did he ask her out if he was here temporarily? Was he looking for a fling?

"You sound disappointed."

"I thought you lived here and maybe worked by Zoom or Teams or something." A long-distance relationship would be difficult. Especially if she got caught up in her work. *Relax, Nora. It's a first date. You aren't engaged.*

"That would be okay. But for a lot of things, in person simply makes sense. It's logical. I'm debating retiring. But I'm not sure I'm ready yet."

"I've heard that retiring is hard for men. Women do their jobs, but men are their jobs. It's harder for them to separate from that lifestyle. Of course, I am my job. Sometimes, painting and sketching are all consuming."

"That's an interesting comment on the life/work balance." He tipped the server when she set their glasses on the table. "What are you working on?"

He seemed genuinely interested. He looked directly at her and kept eye contact, so she answered. "I have several commissions, one of which is a painting of someone's gardens based on a photograph. Though why they want a painting of their gardens escapes me; I can't do it justice like a proper photo would." She shrugged. "Aside from that, I'm working with some pencil sketches. It's different for me. It's a real challenge. I don't sketch much. I can. I just usually go straight for the paints. I'm more comfortable there. I'm working on my drawing skills, but for some reason, paint is easier."

"I'm sure your sketches are fabulous. I'd love to see them sometime."

"Are you asking to come up and see my etchings?" The teasing remark slipped out before she could stop it.

"Are you inviting me?" He winked.

She snatched up her wine and swallowed several mouthfuls. She was tempted. Too tempted. She barely knew him. Okay, she didn't know him at all. She wasn't the type to fall into bed on the first date. Heck, she'd been single for nearly seven years and had yet to sleep with another man. Not because she was heartbroken or mourning her relationship, but because she'd never found anyone who stirred her emotions and libido like Ross did. There was something about his dark hair and blue eyes that drew her in and set her heart tripping.

"Relax," he patted her hand sending shards of sweet arousal prickling through her. "I was joking."

Suddenly, she wanted this. A hot fling with a sexy man. "It would have to be at your place," she flirted. "I have roommates."

"I'm staying with my brother." He groaned. "That sounds so juvenile."

She couldn't help but laugh. "It's okay. Maybe another time." Regret swamped her. "Tell about Florida. Are there lots of gators?"

They talked for hours. First about Florida, then books and movies. There was a weird dynamic between them. Not awkward exactly, but like a humming attraction that wouldn't be denied. She didn't want to focus on it, but her nerve endings seemed hyper attuned to him. They barely acknowledged his brothers and her girlfriends who shared their table. They talked and talked and got to know each other.

"All right. That's it. I'm out," Eve said, interrupting Nora's conversation with Ross. "I need to get some sleep or I'll burn down the studio tomorrow."

Nora pivoted to face her friend. "What time is it?"

"After eleven. You ready to go?" She looked at Nora, then at Cyn.

"Declan will bring me home. You two go on ahead," Cyn said.

Nora didn't feel ready to leave yet. She looked at Ross, silently asking if he was ready to go. He shrugged and smiled.

She'd love to stay and get to know him better, so she said, "I'll take a cab home."

"I'll drive you home," Ross offered. "If Eve can drop off Tom?"

"I can do that. Catch you later," Eve said. After a quick goodbye, the others departed, and Nora and Ross were left alone at the large table.

"More wine?" he asked. "Maybe something else to eat?"

"Both?" She laughed, her earlier nerves resurfacing. She'd had a burger and fries and two glasses of wine. She probably didn't need more of either, but she wanted both, and at this stage of her life, she balanced wants, needs, and desires. And, boy of boy, was she ever feeling desire.

"Excellent." He ordered them a tray of appetizers and more drinks. "Bring the lady a fresh glass of water too, please."

"Water?"

"You should stay hydrated. Statistically speaking, you'll experience less deleterious effects if you drink water while you consume alcohol. I noticed that you're only drinking wine."

"I usually go one water for every glass of wine. Thanks for looking out for me." And…the awkwardness was back.

"You know I'm not judging you, right? I like you. I don't want you to end up with a hangover."

"Thanks." She drank the last of her wine. It felt strange, good-strange, to have a man openly concerned for her well-being.

"Are you going to put your work back in a gallery?"

"I've thought about it. But they take such a large percentage, and I have to attend all the openings, and to be honest, I really don't enjoy them."

"You should consider putting your work out there again. Your reputation is excellent. I think people would flock to your shows."

"I'd put a million miles on my car with all the travel, either that or I'd have to move back to the city. I don't want to leave my daughter."

The idea had potential. Their drinks came and the discussion was dropped. An idea began forming in her mind, she couldn't quite put her finger on it, but she wondered if there was a better way to show her work than shows in the city or just on her website.

Another two glasses of wine and she was beat. She yawned widely. "I think I should go." She'd rather stay and talk to him. The alcohol had taken the edge off her nerves, and she was finally feeling comfortable.

"I'm not in any shape to drive." He grinned. "I drank more than I should have. But I enjoyed being with you and didn't want an empty glass to scare you away. I can call you a cab or walk you home. Your choice?"

She pulled out her phone and punched a few keys. "Weather app says it's only minus two Celsius. I'm good to walk if you are."

Their Christmas Love

Chapter Three

He shouldn't feel giddy that he got to spend more time with Nora, but Ross couldn't help himself. She was easy to talk to once her nerves wore off. They shared the same taste in movies, they both loved action flicks, but he wouldn't be caught dead reading a romance, and she didn't seem inclined towards thrillers.

She had adorable laugh lines around her eyes and mouth. It seemed that she was a woman who enjoyed life. And that dress. It should be outlawed. Nobody should see her in it except him. It wasn't revealing or especially tight. But the fabric must have some astronomical qualities to both cling and float freely at the same time. One moment friction held it tight, the next it slid away like friction didn't exist. With every small motion she made, he was certain he was about to get a glimpse of something…but he never did. It was making him crazy. Her hem had ridden up just enough that he could see the base of her thigh, right above her knee, and it was all he could do not to touch her tempting skin.

"If you're ready, we can go, or stay for another drink." He knew what he wanted, but he'd abide by her wishes.

"Oh. I definitely don't need more alcohol or food. I'm stuffed to the gills. I think I'm ready to call it a night." She stood and pushed back her chair.

"Let me help you with your jacket." He pulled her jacket from the hook beside their table and held it out. She slipped into it, the small motions sending a fresh wave of something fruity toward him. He couldn't put his finger on the precise scent, but it sent his hormones into overdrive. He'd been trying to identify it all night.

She was killing him. Her unique and delicious scent, the way she laughed. The sparkling blue of her eyes. Even the tiny specks of blue and red paint in her hair aroused him. He dropped a few bills on the table to cover the remains of their tab and a generous tip, then offered her his arm.

Her warm smile stole his breath. "This was fun," he said when his brain started working again. "You're good company."

"Thanks. You are too. You're quite easy to talk to." Even if just being near him seemed to scramble her circuits.

They navigated their way between tables and outside into the brisk winter air. Light snow drifted around them and glittered in the streetlights. She slid on her low heels. "Oh. I think I drank more than I realized." She stumbled, and he just managed to catch her shoulders and keep her from falling on her face. His wife had once told him that women sometimes got drunk in a rush. It had something to do with the alcohol capacity of their fat cells. One minute they were fine, the next minute drunk as a sailor. He didn't know if it was true or not, but it seemed so in this case. He made a mental note to research the idea.

"Oh, my hero." She giggled. "Thank you for saving me." She stepped forward and brushed her lips over his.

Sparks exploded in his brain and down his nerve endings. The woman was lethal to his self-control. He took a small step back without releasing her.

"Don't you want to kiss me? I want to kiss you. I've wanted to taste your handsome lips all night." Another giggle.

He knew she wasn't sober, but he hadn't realized she was this drunk. Maybe he should get a taxi rather than walking her home. He was debating the idea when her arms snaked around his neck and she pulled his head lower.

"Kiss me, Ross. I need another taste."

How the hell was a man supposed to resist that? "Mm." He brushed his lips across hers. She tasted of wine and the sweet apple pie she'd finished the evening with. Below those tastes was the heady flavor that was uniquely Nora. Divine. The air was cold, but his body burned with need.

Her tongue darted out, brushing his lips, urging them to open. Unbidden, his mouth opened and his tongue danced with hers. This was all sorts of wrong. He needed to back away. To put distance between them. Now. His glasses steamed up from their heat.

His arms wrapped around her waist, pulling her closer. She was luscious against him. Soft, warm, pliable. Curvy and delicious. She was heaven in his arms. She moaned and squirmed closer. His senses exploded to life. His body hardened. He wanted her. Here. Now. He was rapidly losing control of his sanity and inhibitions.

Reluctantly, he pulled back. He put his fogged-up glasses into his pocket. "As much as I'm enjoying this, it's too cold out here, and we've both had too much to drink."

"You're rejecting me?" She stumbled backward, crossing her arms over her chest, unknowingly emphasizing her cleavage. He tried not to stare. Instead, he reached out and buttoned her jacket, carefully avoiding touching her.

"Not at all, beautiful. I'm so hard I can hardly think. I'm saying not here. Not now. Later. You deserve more than a quick tryst in the snow."

"Oh." The word was a breath and a whimper. "Okay. I guess."

31

She was an adorable drunk, and he would not take advantage of her. Ever. "Come on, Nora, let's get you home." He slipped his arm around her waist and turned her around.

Her arm snaked behind his, and she pulled him closer. "Okay." She giggled. "But can we do *it* later?"

"Anything you want; and soon. Very soon. I don't know how long I can resist you." He reached across her and took her right hand in his left. It could have been awkward, to walk holding hands across their bodies with their arms wrapped around each other's waist. But it felt nice. Cozy. And it gave him the best leverage to keep her upright on the slippery sidewalks.

"The snow is pretty." She paused to look at the falling flakes. "It's supposed to be good luck to catch a flake on your tongue." She stuck her tongue out.

"Is it?" *What the heck? He hadn't done anything fun in ages.* He stuck his out too.

"Make a wish," she mumbled around her tongue.

A wish? What did a grown man wish for? He didn't need anything. Except to get to know Nora better, and maybe take her to bed. Not casually, but as the start to something lasting. He was done with casual relationships and ready to move on to something permanent. Nora was smart, pretty, talented, just the right kind of woman. Spending more time with her and learning all her quirks seemed like the perfect wish.

"I got one!" she exclaimed just as a flake landed on his tongue.

"Me too. What did you wish for?" he asked.

"Nope. Nope. You can't share your wish or it won't come true." She waggled her finger at him. "You have to let the universe act on your wish." Her words weren't slurred, but there was a hint of the alcohol she consumed in them.

Wishing on snowflakes was superstitious nonsense. His logical mind struggled with believing. In the end, he kept his unvocalized wish to himself. Somewhere, deep inside, he figured what the heck, it wouldn't hurt to try and believe.

"Come on then, my little artist, let's get you home." With a gentle tug, they started forward.

"What's your biggest dream?" she asked, sounding slightly less tipsy. Perhaps the cool weather was sobering her up, or maybe it was the simple act of moving.

"I don't know that I've thought about it," he said. "As a teenager, I wanted to work for NASA. I've done that. I love my work. I'm happy there. How about you?"

"Can you keep a secret?" She frowned.

"Always. Your secrets are safe with me." A couple hours and she was sharing secrets? Maybe she was tipsier than she seemed.

"I want to be happy again. I'm not unhappy, but I'm not happy either. I'm..." She paused. "I'm lonely. But don't tell Cyn and Eve that. I don't want them to know. They're my best friends, but I can't tell them everything." They walked another half block. "You're easy to talk to. You weren't at first. You make me all fidgety and nervous. You make me want hot steamy kisses in the dark. I want to drag you into the park and make love to you on the bench. In public. Right now. But don't tell anyone."

Jeepers. How was he supposed to react to that? "Again, your secrets are safe with me. I'm sorry you're lonely." His heart squeezed knowing this beautiful,

34

friendly woman didn't have everything she needed to make her heart happy.

"I'm tired, can we sit for a minute?" They were crossing behind the elementary school yard and close to the swings.

"Do you promise not to ravish me?" he teased.

"Nope."

He helped her into a swing and gave her a small push, careful not to send the swing too high lest she tumble out. "Tell me about your wish." He couldn't stop himself from insisting. He needed to know.

"I wish I had been enough of a woman for my ex. I wish I could have kept him." Her voice was low and almost unintelligible. He wondered if he'd heard her right.

"He was an idiot to let you go. Do you still love him?" *Please say no.*

"Dickhead? Don't tell him I call him that. Do I love him? Nope. I mean, I love him like a friend and as the father of my child. But as a woman loves a man? That deep passionate, hungry, needy, lustful love. You know the kind, where you can't wait to be with them in every sense, especially naked. Do I still feel that for him? Not one bit. We're over."

She took a deep breath. "I want a man who sees me for who I am. One who accepts my artist quirks and understands that when the muse calls, I have to listen. Art is my soul. I need someone who understands that. I'm fifty-three. I don't need to play games. I won't. Does that make sense?"

"It does. I'm fifty-four. I don't want to be chasing women around. I want someone stable who will be there for me and support me no matter where my career or retirement take me. I want someone to travel with and to sleep beside at night. I want someone who brings me peace and passion." Holy crap! Where had that come from? He didn't know he felt that way until this moment, and he sure hadn't meant to spring it on her.

"That's beautiful." She stopped the swing. "Come home with me, Ross. Just one night together?"

He helped her off the swing. He'd take her home, but he sure wasn't going to spend the night with her. He wasn't that guy. But sober, he'd go with her in a heartbeat. "Lead the way, beautiful lady." He followed her instructions and had her home in minutes. He walked her upstairs to her room and sat her on the side of her bed.

"Let's get naked," she declared.

"Lay back and I'll take those damp socks off." Her socks were dripping water. He hadn't realized she had stepped in some of the many puddles they'd passed. If he had realized how much the earlier snow had melted and turned to slush, they'd have taken a cab. Her poor feet must be frozen.

She lay back, and he slowly peeled her socks off. Her feet were lovely. Ruby painted toenails. Creamy soft skin. He rubbed them between his hands until they warmed up and turned soft pink instead of icy white.

His mind wandered to what the rest of her was like. *Down, boy.* He rose and looked down at her. Sound asleep. He stifled a laugh. He didn't want to wake her. Carefully, he eased her up the bed and tucked her in.

She'd probably regret her actions tomorrow, and probably her confession as well. If she remembered either. He stared at her for several minutes until it began to feel inappropriate. Then he tiptoed down the stairs and walked back to Declan's house. Sleep was a long time coming.

Their Christmas Love

Chapter Four

Nora woke with a Marine drum corps pounding behind her eyes. "Ugh, how much did I drink?" She replayed the night in her head. Everyone had gone home, leaving her and Ross alone in the noisy pub. They'd ordered food and another drink. Then more food. And more drink? She couldn't be certain of that last one. Holy cow. She stumbled to the bathroom and found some headache pills. What had she been thinking? It had been years since she'd tied one on. Not since her drunken rages when Dickhead left her. Of course, she'd gotten over that betrayal, but she might not survive this headache.

Coffee. She'd never get moving if she didn't load up on caffeine. She took the world's fastest shower. Her body wanted to stay under the water longer, but her pounding head demanded she get out. She changed into sweats before heading to the kitchen. What was on the agenda today? Not going to town, that was for sure. She might run into Ross. She'd stay home until she heard he'd left town. She'd love to see him again…except she couldn't be sure exactly what she'd said and done last night.

She dashed off a quick text. Surely Cyn would keep her updated so she didn't have to risk accidentally bumping into him.

Her phone rang almost as soon as she hit send. She winced at the volume. Note to self: Put phone on vibrate before you go out drinking. She glanced at the display. The library. Great. Now she'd have to explain herself to Cynthia in person.

"Hey, Nora. Why do you need to know when Ross leaves? Did you do something stupid last night?" Cyn asked. Sometimes having friends who knew everything about you was a pain in the backside.

"I don't want to talk about it. And keep it down, my head is killing me."

"How much did you drink?" Cyn's voice was low, but still added a bugle band to the drum chorus in Nora's head. "And what did you do that you need to avoid Ross? Don't you screw up my chance at a relationship with Declan."

"I won't screw anything up. Just let me know when Ross goes back to Florida. I'm staying home until then. I'll explain it all later."

"Explain what later?" Eve asked, strolling into the room dressed in a crop top and yoga pants. Her shiny brunette hair was pulled into a high ponytail. "I won't be around later. I've got to teach the seniors' yoga class at the community center, then I'm heading out to the studio. I've got a great idea for a snowman sculpture using aluminum cans." She rented warehouse space on the outskirts of town. Working with metal and welders wasn't something you could do just anywhere; it required plenty of space and proper ventilation.

"I got drunk last night. Stupid, high school drunk. I don't remember coming home. The only blessing is that I was still dressed when I woke up." She groaned. "I'm mortified."

"Put me on speaker," Cyn demanded. After Nora complied, she said, "At least you were dressed." She laughed. "What was with you? I tried to catch your eye and get you to slow down, but you totally ignored me."

"And me," Eve added. "You were pounding wine back like a woman out of control."

"Don't remind me." She set the phone on the counter and put a filter in the coffee pot. No pods this morning, she'd need the entire pot. "I was so nervous. He's so hot, and so smart, and that gray at his temples...wow. And those glasses. Wow. I thought a drink would help. It did, at first. But booze has a way of...deleting my inhibitions." Heat flooded her face. "I damn near crawled into his lap."

"Yeah, we saw that." Eve laughed and poured herself a glass of Kombucha, the fermented tea she liked. "Want some? I'll cure your headache."

"No, thanks. I don't remember much after you guys left. More food, more wine." An image flooded her mind. Crap. No way. She didn't. "Oh my god, I think I kissed him."

"What?" her friends shouted in unison.

"You didn't," Cyn groaned, obviously thinking about her burgeoning relationship with Ross's brother.

"I think I did," she whispered, mortified. "What was I thinking?"

42

"Shoot, someone's coming to the desk, I have to go. We'll finish this discussion when I get home." Cyn clicked off.

"And I'm running late for yoga. We'll talk after work. Go paint something, work that stress off. Put all that unspent passion into your art."

As fast as that, she was alone. Abandoned by her friends. She didn't know whether to be annoyed or grateful. She grabbed her coffee and headed upstairs to her studio in the bonus room over the garage. Sunlight streamed in, blinding her and making a mockery of her headache which seemed to taunt her about her mistakes. The bright colorful room was usually an inspiration; today, it was depressing. The emotions and thoughts she'd put into her art mocked her tired brain.

Moving slowly, she walked past her main easel and client commissions and pulled a stool up to her drafting board. She didn't use it for drafting, but the tiltable table made it easy to sketch. She could paint, but something about knowing she could erase pencil was soothing in her current state of mind. She'd love to erase half of last night. She picked up her largest sketchbook and turned it to a fresh page. She had no idea what she was going to draw, but rudimentary drawing always relieved her tension.

And she was tense.

She fumbled through her pencils and charcoal sticks, finally settling on a soft lead pencil. She closed off the thrumming thoughts in her mind and shut her eyes. Several slow deep breaths of the lingering smell of paint and turpentine mingled with coffee brought a measure of calm. This was her happy place; the place where she fed her soul.

She opened her eyes. The bright colors of her paintings exploded into her mind, bringing a frisson of excitement now that she was less tense. This was where she needed to be. A few sips of coffee, and she was ready. She set her mind free and let it direct her pencil. The first mark was a startlingly bold slash across the paper. Her brow wrinkled as she stared at it.

What the heck?

It didn't matter. This was for stress reduction, not for payment. She had no intention of anyone ever seeing what was in her sketchbooks. They were for her and her alone. She could draw whatever her muse threw at her.

Her subconscious pushed her hand and she drew a few more lines, a couple curves. Faster and faster her hand moved. Before her eyes, and against her will, an image formed.

Ross.

He was outside, in the dark, lit only by the glow of a streetlight. He was surrounded by falling snow. The image was sweet and romantic. A memory exploded into her mind. Sticking her tongue out, catching snowflakes. Making wishes. Making confessions of her deepest dreams to a man she hardly knew.

No! She didn't. Did she?

Her stomach plummeted and bounced up alarmingly.

She couldn't have. No way.

The scene played out in her mind. She had tried, again and again, to seduce him. Gallantly, he'd refused. Then, she'd confessed her deepest fears and dreams. No wonder he wasn't there when she woke up. He was probably halfway to Florida or the Cayman Islands by now.

Her stomach roiled, the coffee and pain meds gurgling dangerously. She should eat.

She turned the page and started fresh. She'd draw her friends. Cyn came first, then Eve. Then her daughter, Melissa. Each taking a place in the collage forming on the rough drawing sheet. She sharpened her pencil and kept going. Micro-sketches of pets she'd had. Her ex. Then Ross.

Ross? Again?

She squeezed the pencil in both hands, willing his image to disappear from the page.

Snap!

She stared down at the broken pencil. Dang it! Good quality pencils weren't cheap. She wasn't broke, not by a long shot, but she hated waste. She'd use the halves until they were nubs. She put one end back in the container and honed the point on the other piece.

She flipped the page again and sat staring at the accusingly blank paper for five minutes. Rebelliously, she shut her creative mind away and began to mechanically draw a forest scene.

Trees, a wandering stream. Flowers. She shaded and filled in the forest, adding detail after detail. When the page was full, she leaned back and squinted her eyes at the picture. It was good. A hawk soared; squirrels hid in the trees. Deer lingered in the background. There was an image hiding below all that.

It was Ross.

What? How?

Somehow, despite ignoring her muse, Ross had crept into the picture. Nobody but her would notice him, but he was there in the depths and shadows. This wasn't her usual work. It was different, and she had to admit that it was good. Probably sellable. It reminded her of those drawings where one animal morphed into another, only this was more subtle. It was also her brain sending her a message. She needed to talk to Ross.

Resolved, she put down the pencil, hid her sketchbook away, and shut off the lights. She didn't have his number, but she knew where he lived.

Her stomach growled. Either from worry or hunger. Okay, food first, then off to face the dragon. Except he wasn't the problem in this case; she was. It sucked because he was a nice guy. Caring, funny, easy to talk to...once she got over her nerves. With luck, he wouldn't think she was an idiot, or a tart.

Tart. Mm. She could use a tart. New order of business. A banana to calm her stomach, an apology to Ross, then the bakery for a tart and maybe a cinnamon bun.

Chapter Five

Fifteen minutes later, bundled against the weather, she stood on Ross's brother Declan's front step. At least she hoped it was his house. She was nearly certain that this was the right place. She knocked. And waited. After the third round of knocks, she tried the doorbell. It rang with a melodic chime audible through the door.

Inside the house, someone cussed and the sound of footsteps approached. The door flew open. "Yeah?"

Ross stood there, dripping wet, clutching a towel around his waist.

Holy sugar bananas. What sweet heaven was this?

"Hi." *Nice inane greeting.*

"Nora! Hi. I wasn't expecting you." His smile lit his eyes.

"Yeah, I gathered that. Sorry to bother you." *Not sorry to see him nearly naked.*

"Come in. It's freezing out there." His skin puckered up with goosebumps, and he shivered. He waved her inward, not releasing his grip on the slipping towel.

She could barely draw her eyes away from the temptation. He shut the door behind her. Nervous, she inhaled deeply. Mistake. He smelled fresh, squeaky clean, like soap. His five o'clock shadow drew her gaze. It would feel amazing against her skin. She curled her toes and clenched her hands together to keep from moving in for a taste of those luscious lips.

"What can I do for you?" His smile made her knees weak. He didn't seem bothered by his near nudity.

"Um. Ya. I came to apologize." She should have planned her words before she got here. This was crazy. She swallowed to relieve the dryness in her throat.

"Apologize for what?" He winked. "For falling asleep while I was taking your shoes off?"

"Oh, no! Tell me I didn't." *He'd come in the house and taken her shoes off?* Crap. Those shoes were still on her bedroom floor. He'd been in her…bedroom? She nearly swooned with mortification. "I don't remember much. I'm sorry I got wasted like a teenager. I'm not impulsive like that. It was an off night."

"It's okay. Everyone has rough days."

A drop of water trailed down his chest; she watched it until it disappeared under the towel. She would not lick the water droplets from his incredible abs.

"How about I go get dressed and we can talk about it?"

"Um. Yeah. Sure. That would be great." She'd rather stare at his naked chest than discuss last night, but if it meant staying with him longer, she was game. At least he hadn't ridiculed her or thrown her out of the house. Small victories. She couldn't recall ever being this nervous, except at her first gallery showing where she was sure nobody would show up.

He walked away; her gaze stuck to his retreating form like her eyes had been glued there. The man was built like an athlete, not a mathematician. She took half a step before realizing she was trailing after him. Not good.

She stood in the entry hall, peering into the living area while she waited. Ross's brothers kept a tidy house, at least from this angle. The living room had two leather couches angled toward the enormous television over the fireplace. The carpet looked plush and soft.

"Okay then. Why don't you come in? Sorry I didn't ask you sooner." He smiled and made a come-in gesture. "Let me take your coat."

Did she want to come in? Come closer? Her mind said no. Her libido said YES! "Sure. I was heading to the bakery after this, but I can stay for a minute."

"I can cook for you; if you're hungry."

She was hungry alright, but not for food. "You don't have to go to that much trouble." She could just nibble on him. She mentally taped up her lust and shoved into the darkest recess of her mind where it belonged. *Focus on the conversation, not his hot, sexy body.*

Her stomach growled, distracting her from her naughty thoughts.

"Food it is, and it's no trouble. I was just going to eat. Of course, I probably would have eaten toast and cereal. Cooking for one isn't much fun. I'd rather cook for both of us. Sausages and waffles okay with you?"

"You can cook? I mean, sausages and waffles will be amazing. Thank you." She slipped out of her jacket, and he hung it on the wooden coat rack. She put her boots neatly at the edge of the mat.

"Come on then, into the kitchen, where you can confess all your sins." His light tone let her know that whatever she might have done last night, he wasn't upset by it. Whew!

The floor was warm under her feet. "Is the floor heated?"

He laughed at her surprise. "It is, and I can tell you that heated floors are the world's greatest invention. Full stop. No exceptions. I'd freeze to death up here without them."

"Um, should you get dressed? Not that I'm not enjoying the view." *Did she have to say that?*

"Right. Okay. Be right back." He backed out of the kitchen, leaving her standing in the middle of the tidy room.

He was back in under three minutes. She wanted to run her fingers through his damp hair. Maybe to smooth it, maybe to yank him closer for a kiss.

"Coffee?" He held up the pot in question.

"That would be good." *Anything to distract her from thinking about kisses in the shower.* "I'm nursing a bit of a hangover." Might as well get the discussion underway. The sooner she started, the sooner it was done. "Cream and sugar, please."

"I've got Kahlua if you want the hair of the dog that bit you."

"No! I think I still have enough booze in my system to last me a week." She laughed. Maybe it wasn't quite that bad, but the idea of alcohol this early, and before eating, landed in her stomach with a nauseating thud. "Cream and sugar would be nice."

He passed the cream and sugar over and bustled around the kitchen pulling out pans and an electric waffle iron. He didn't pressure her with conversation, which actually made opening up harder. Finally, half a cup of coffee later, she spoke.

"Look, Ross. I'm sorry I drank too much last night. I'm not usually like that. I rarely drink. Honestly, you make me nervous. It's been years since I went on a date of any kind. At fifty-three, I'm out of practice. I didn't handle myself well. I apologize. It won't happen again."

"It's okay. I understand. I was rather nervous myself. I'm a nerd, so I rarely go out except with the other nerds at work. Dating is rare for me too. First off, I was a single father of twin boys, and I was busy with everything they needed. It wasn't until they moved away to join the army that I realized how solitary my life had become."

"It does sort of creep up on you, doesn't it?" She understood exactly what he meant. "When Melissa started school, I realized how much time I devoted to her. Not that I minded. I loved every second, but I soon discovered that I didn't have anyone, except myself and my girlfriends. They're great, but they aren't the be-all and end-all of my life. I'm looking for someone who is interested in a serious relationship." Oops. She hadn't meant to confess that. Hadn't she done enough damage spilling all her secrets last night?

Ross flipped off the stove and turned to face her. His chest rose and fell with an enormous breath. She froze, waiting for the rejection she knew was coming. "Nora, I like you. A lot. You're funny, you're talented. You're beautiful. But I have to be honest. I live in Florida. I love my job. I am looking for a long-term relationship, but the person needs to know the truth of my life. I can't always be around."

"I see." She did understand, but she wasn't sure what he was driving at.

His brows knit together. "What I'm saying is, I am interested in seeing where this goes with you, with our eyes on long-term, not just a fling. But you need to be aware that I'm in and out of Valley Springs a lot. I'm not sure how often I'll be able to come back once my vacation is over."

"I can live with that." She smiled as her heart pounded out a happy beat.

"Good. Then come over here and give me the kiss you kept trying to foist off on me last night. It took everything I had not to accept what you were offering."

Head rose in her face. She was hoping he'd forget. She licked her lips and nibbled the lower one, trying to work up the courage.

"Stop teasing me." He winked. "I'm dying for a taste." He crooked his finger in a come-here motion, and like a puppet on a string, she went to him.

His hands went to her hips. His head titled left, his eyes held questions and the spark of desire. "Good morning, Nora." He inched forward. She went up on her toes to meet him. His lips brushed hers. Jolts of electricity flooded her veins, bringing her nerve endings to life. Heat pooled low in her belly. Her heart went pitta-pat.

Holy sugar bananas. The man was lethal. She pressed toward him, deepening the kiss.

"Not so fast," he whispered against her lips. "I'm struggling to maintain control here. I spent the entire night fantasizing about the dress you wore last night. All I could think about was stripping you out of it."

A giggle escaped her. Mission accomplished. She might be in her fifties, but she still had needs. She wasn't young and foolish. She knew what she wanted, and right now, and just like last night, she needed Ross.

A million thoughts exploded through her mind, each battling for control. She pushed them aside and toyed with the buttons on her blouse. She should eat. She should leave. She leaned into him and whispered in his ear.

Their Christmas Love

58

Chapter Six

Ross leaned back and stared at Nora. He couldn't have heard her correctly. He swallowed the lump in his throat. "I beg your pardon?"

"I said, do you want to show me your bedroom?" She flicked open one of her buttons, revealing an enticing patch of skin and a tiny heart necklace. His heart jumped.

"I thought you said you were hungry." This was a joke. It had to be. Sexy women didn't come on to nerdy mathematicians. Not in real life. He pushed up his glasses and started solving a quadratic equation in his head to distract himself from the alluring display in front of him.

"I am hungry." She licked her lips. "You first, food later." A hint of color slipped over her cheeks. She wasn't as confident as she sounded. Her nerves reassured him.

"Are you certain?" *God, don't let her change her mind now. I'm rock hard and ready.* "I don't want to push you into anything."

She took him by the hand and pulled him toward the kitchen door. "Come on, Ross. Before I chicken out. Life's too short to worry over little things. Just being with you turns me on. We're both consenting adults. Come play with me." She gave his hand a tug.

Speechless, he doubled checked that the burners and waffle iron were off, led her upstairs and into the guest bedroom. Thank heaven both his brothers were gone for the day. He closed the door and leaned against it. His knees trembled. What was it about Nora that affected him so strongly? He'd been half tongue tied the day they met. If she hadn't kept the conversation going by asking questions, he'd have stood there like an idiot.

Right now, she was inviting him into his bed, with the potential for a long-term relationship, and he was half tempted to refuse in case he blew it. He didn't want to mess up his chance with her, but he was man enough to know that opportunities like this didn't come along often. Often? How about never?

"Are you joining me?" She sat on the edge of the bed and undid another button.

Sweet heaven! His gaze locked on to her cleavage.

"Don't leave hanging, Ross." Her brow furrowed, and she looked nervous.

He counted to one hundred, by thirteens. To hell with it. If this was what she wanted, he'd give it to her. "Hold still," he said. "I want to memorize this picture. You, on my bed, looking as sexy as hell. Wanting me. I never want to forget this moment." Pink stained her cheeks, and she closed her eyes.

"You've got five seconds," she whispered. Flick…another button opened revealing the valley between her breasts. His patience snapped and he strode to her side.

"You win. I'm helpless to resist."

"Resistance is futile," she quipped.

"You know *Star Trek*?"

She laughed. "I adore *Star Trek*. Climb aboard, Captain, this ship is leaving orbit." She scooted up the bed and lay on her side, head propped on her elbow, the pose pure centerfold.

When had he ever seen anything so enticing? He slipped off his belt and joined her. "Now, in the interest of interplanetary relations, how can I serve you?" he whispered into the curve of her neck.

"I require a full planetary search mission."

He swallowed hard. "Are we investigating your planet, or mine?" He kissed his way down the gap in her blouse. She smelled so good, like lilacs and chocolate. He wanted to devour her.

"This planet has a clothing taboo," she whispered. "All clothing must go, starting with this." She tugged at his T-shirt. "Lose it before the locals get angry." She helped him pull the shirt off and stroked the muscles of his chest. "You're beautiful." She flicked her tongue over his nipple. It hardened instantly and he groaned. "I want to paint you."

He'd never been more grateful for the hours he spent in the gym at work. "You are entirely too well clothed." He opened her buttons, slowly, kissing every inch of skin as it came into view. "You have the perfect hourglass figure. Probably the perfect esthetic proportions."

"Are you going all math nerd on me?" She giggled.

"Do you like it?" he teased, half worried that his inner nerd was showing too much.

"That depends on the length of your measuring rod." She cupped his groin. "Show me what you've got, NASA man. Take me to your rocket and fly me to the moon."

He laughed at the unusual bedroom talk.

"Are you laughing at me?" she asked. He was kissing her abdomen, but heard the laugh in her voice.

"Yes. A little. The hypotenuse is the longest side of a right-angle triangle." He unfastened her jeans and kissed lower. She lifted her hips so he could slide them down.

"Oh, tell me more." She gasped when he pulled her jeans off and cast them aside. He nuzzled the soft skin of her stomach just about her half-off panties. Pink silk!

"More?" He could barely think, she was so intoxicating. "The hypotenuse is the side opposite the right angle. The Pythagorean theorem states that the square of the length of the hypotenuse equals the sum of the squares of the lengths of the other two sides." He kissed her between every word, slowly inching her panties down with his mouth until she was laid bare before him. So beautiful, so sexy, so perfect.

"Poetry is music. Music is mathematical," he whispered against her fragrant thigh. "Your body is poetry, pure mathematical perfection." He couldn't keep the random connections from forming in his over-stimulated brain.

Gently, he spread her legs and lowered his mouth. She cried out and clutched his shoulders at the first touch. This was heaven!

Chapter Seven

A short time later, Nora rolled off Ross and flopped breathlessly beside him on the bed. "Oh my gosh, that was amazing."

He rolled to face her and cupped her cheek in his hand. His eyes were soft with unidentifiable emotion. "No, you are amazing. Be right back." He climbed off the bed and entered the adjoining bathroom. Water ran. Two minutes later, he strode back to the bed, condom free and gloriously naked.

"I really do want to paint you." Something about him was so compelling, she was tempted to propose. She barely knew him, and she had the weirdest feeling that she was in love with him.

He sat on the edge of the bed. "Here, let me clean you up." He held up a damp cloth.

Heat flooded her face. "You don't have to do that. I can wash up." She glanced away from him, both uncomfortable with and thrilled by his caring.

"But I want to." She closed her eyes and parted her legs. The cloth was perfectly warm. Not too hot or too cold. She recited the primary colors in her head. Then the secondary.

"What's that? You're mumbling."

"Nothing."

"I could have sworn I heard colors," he teased, lying beside her.

"You know you're doing too many drugs when you can hear colors," she bantered.

"It's a well-documented fact that you're like a drug to me. I'm high on the pleasure of your company." He tossed the cloth onto the carpet and lay beside her.

"Now there's a corny line."

He pulled her tight to his side and urged her to face away so he was spooning her back. They fit perfectly together. He was warm, but not overly hot against her back. His arm slipped around her waist as he cuddled her.

"Not a line at all," he whispered, his breath tickling her shoulder. "One hundred percent cold hard fact. Now tell me why you were reciting the color wheel?"

She wanted to go into this relationship with complete honesty, but it was hard to tell him the truth. She lay silent, working up her courage. "Because I find it embarrassing that you cleaned me up. Nice, but uncomfortable." She held her breath waiting for him to laugh or say something rude. Her ex had hated this type of confession.

"Never be uncomfortable with me. Not in what you say, or in what you or we do. You are beautiful, your passion was breathtaking. I helped make that lovely mess; I'll help clean it up." He groaned. "That sounded awful. What I meant to say is that after the beautiful moments we shared, I was happy to make your more comfortable. I disposed of the condom and cleaned myself up; why wouldn't you deserve the same, or better?"

"Thank you. Nobody's ever done that for me before." She blushed at the confession. The aftermath of their loving was awkwardly sweet.

"What? They should have. What man makes love to his woman and doesn't treat her like a princess afterward? A jackass, that's who." He snuggled into her. "Can I bring you breakfast?"

"Don't be silly." She rolled over to face him. "We can make it together, but I do appreciate the thought."

"Why don't you nap, and I'll bring you breakfast in bed?" He kissed her forehead and rolled off the bed. "Don't go away, beautiful. Breakfast will be served in fifteen minutes." He pulled a pair of navy sweatpants over his naked backside and slipped on a T-shirt. He blew her a kiss and left, closing the door behind him.

She stared at the white six-panel door for a moment wondering if he was avoiding her. "Nonsense, that's your insecurity talking." She wasn't sleepy, she was invigorated, so a nap was out of the question. She rose and took a quick shower before following him downstairs.

"Hey," he greeted her. "I said I'd bring breakfast up to you." He gave her a one-arm hug as he tended the sausages and bacon on the stove.

"I couldn't wait." She snitched a slice of bacon off the paper towel he was draining it on. "Mm. Delicious. Perfect crispness. Do I smell fresh coffee?"

"You do. Help yourself. I take cream and sugar in mine, if you don't mind pouring for both of us." He flashed her a grin.

"Are you always this genial?" He seemed unusually courteous, not that her ex was anyone to judge behavior by.

Ross paused thoughtfully. "Honestly, I don't know. Something about you makes me want to be extra nice. It's been a long time since I had a girlfriend. I want to be certain I treat you right so you know I care when I'm off to Florida, or lost in a math problem." He shrugged and smiled.

"I appreciate it." She didn't want to think about him leaving. They'd just met, and sex with him was out of this world. She'd had not one, but four orgasms. She couldn't even do that to herself and she knew exactly where to touch. She turned away from him, pretending to be busy with their coffee. She didn't want him to see her enormous smile. Damn, the man could make love. If she wasn't worried about looking like a tramp, she'd seduce him again.

"You're thinking very hard. Want to share? Or is that pushing my limits? I know women don't always want to discuss their post-coital thoughts." He popped down some toast and cracked eggs into the frying pan.

69

"I suppose that's true. It's not always easy to open up, and we're practically strangers."

"Intimate strangers. I want to get to know you better. I only have today and tomorrow. I fly home on Monday, but I'll be back for Winterfest."

"Oh." She hated that her disappointment was obvious.

"Can I give you my home, cell, and work numbers? My email? I'd like to talk to you while I'm gone. A lot. Maybe every day?" He put a lid on the egg pan and faced her. "No pressure though."

She clasped her hands behind her back and squeezed her fingers together to keep from grabbing him into a hug. "I'd like that." She set the table then went to the front door to grab her phone. She unlocked it and handed it to him. "Why don't you put yourself in? Then I'll text you and you'll have my number. I only have one. No house phone or office." The exchange was quick and efficient, and they sat down to eat.

"What shall we do today? Do I need to step aside for your muse?" He sounded like he actually understood her muse and wasn't jealous of her need to create.

"No work today, at least not yet. I have to go to Whitefalls. They've got a great art store. I need some watercolors. Usually, I work in oil, but I have this urge to get back to watercolors, and I'm short on cerulean blue and about six other colors. Want to go with me?"

"Sure. I'd like that. I'll buy you lunch."

She laughed. "We aren't even finished with breakfast."

"I'll have you know that I intend to work it off you later." He winked and turned his gaze back to his plate.

"Indeed? Tell me more, Mr. Mathematician."

He did, in glorious detail, until she was worried that she'd have to take him right there on the table. "Maybe Whitefalls can wait." The man had a way with words. Without being brutally graphic, he'd painted an erotic picture she couldn't get out of her mind.

"No, it cannot. I've used up my entire supply of condoms."

"You call two condoms a supply?"

"Honestly? I stole those from Tom. He'll probably have a fit if he notices. I don't carry them as a rule. I snuck them yesterday, before our date."

"Planning on seducing someone?" she teased, not really upset.

"While the odds of making love to you on our first date were astronomically against me, I was hoping that against those odds, I might bring you home with me. I had no designs on anyone else. I swear." He crossed his heart and grinned.

Chapter Eight

Ross stood in the bright winter sunshine staring down at Nora's emerald green Honda Civic. It suited her. Colorful, vibrant, sleek curves. "Cute car."

"Hey, don't knock it. The price was right. It gets great gas mileage, and it's great on the highway in winter. What do you drive?"

"There's a bit of snow, and I'm not used to winter driving. I'll let you chauffeur us today. I don't actually own a vehicle. I'm close to transit, and I carpool to work. Everything I need is close. When I come visit here, I rent a car in Edmonton or take the bus here from the airport. Owning a car would be a waste for me. Though I can see why you'd need one here."

"Actually, I rarely drive. I walk a lot and take the car for groceries. Valley Springs is small enough to get around easily. Shall we?" She beeped the doors open and climbed in. She was graceful and watching her was addicting; it feed something in him, he hadn't known was hungry.

They chatted about food and movies on the forty-minute drive to Whitefalls. She was easy to talk to and had several insightful comments on the subtext of the movies they watched. "I don't mind a message, all good stories have them, but sometimes, movies just seem bent on beating you over the head with a lecture on something. What happened to subtle?" She pulled to a stop in front of the art store. "Here we are." She turned to face him. "I warn you; this might take a while. I'm easily distracted by the tools of my trade."

"No worries. I'm happy to hang out and wait."

The proprietor of the store greeted them eagerly. "Nora! I'm so glad to see you. You haven't been in for a while. I was starting to worry that you'd given up art." The petite, gray-haired owner drew Nora into her embrace. Ross laughed at himself for feeling jealous of someone who reminded him of Edna Mode from *The Incredibles*.

"Not at all. I've been focused on oils and sketching." She dug in her purse. "I've got a list of what I need. I'll grab this stuff and look around. Oh, this is my friend, Ross."

"Ross, eh?" She raised an eyebrow, making him wonder exactly what she was thinking. "Nice to meet you, Ross." She turned back to Nora. "I can get the list, if you want to browse."

"That would be great." Nora passed over the paper. "I'll also need a canvas delivery. The numbers and sizes are on the back. I'd appreciate it if you could ship them to me. I'm okay with waiting for the whole order. I know the fifty by sixty and other large ones are special order."

"That's a big canvas," Ross piped in.

"Sometimes, I paint large." She laughed though she seemed completely serious.

"We just got a shipment of wood plaques. Three by three and four by four. Ready to hang, if you've got a hankering for miniatures."

The conversation went on and on. It was interesting to get a glimpse inside the artist's mind. Especially since Nora was the artist in question. He followed her around the store. Up and down aisles. He never would have guessed the store would hold so many treasures. Pencils, canvases, and about twenty kinds of paints in solid, liquid, oil, water-based. Paint even came in chemical and organic versions. Frankly, he was astounded and fascinated. Some of it seemed reasonably priced, but the organic? He calculated one brand at ninety dollars an ounce. Prices like that weren't for the faint of heart.

Nora picked up ten little pots of the organic. "I've been waiting for these," she told him. "I had a sample pot, and I have the perfect project to try them with."

Try them? Who practiced with supplies that costly? He realized that she must be more affluent that she seemed. Either that or her passion was out of control. Eventually, he hoped to learn which; for today, he was content to be her shadow and carry her shopping basket. He was already dreading going home to Florida without her.

Idly, he wondered if she'd consider moving to Florida. He stopped dead in his tracks. What was he thinking? Permanency? He barely knew her. A couple conversations over wine and a few good orgasms—okay, great orgasms—wasn't enough to build a relationship on.

All day he watched her. She was kind and generous with the staff of the stores they entered. She could converse with anyone. She took delight in small children, bright colors, and all types of flowers and foliage. He could have watched her for days.

Ross dropped his suitcase in the front entry of his condo. He was exhausted. With three weather delays and two re-routings, his trip home had taken thirty-six hours. He definitely wasn't making it in to work today. He could barely keep his eyes open. He never had been able to sleep on planes or in airports. He dashed a text off to Declan and Tom, letting them know he'd made it. Then, he poured himself a small shot of Glenmorangie and climbed into bed. He couldn't even be bothered to shower. He'd change the sheets tomorrow. Smiling to himself, he texted Nora.

Ross: Made it home at long last.

Nora: Glad you're home safe. I was getting worried.

He couldn't help but smile. He sipped his whiskey.

Ross: What are you doing?

Nora: Heading into the studio. You?

Ross: Sitting in my bed, drinking whiskey.

She sent back a shot glass emoji and a coffee cup one.

Nora: It's coffee time here. Seems early for alcohol. It's ten a.m. here.

Ross: Not after the last thirty-six hours it doesn't. Even if it is only eight. I haven't slept for over forty-five hours. I'm bushed. I'm too old for these delays. Headed to bed now. Talk to you later. Tomorrow. Or whenever I wake up.

Nora: Sleep well. Sweet dreams.

The kiss emoji she sent went straight to his groin.

Ross: Thanks.

Nora: You're supposed to go to sleep after someone says sweet dreams.

Ross: But I like talking to you. (Grin emoji.)

Nora: Good night, Ross. Zzzzz.

Smiling, he chugged the last of his Scotch and lay down in a beam of sunlight that flooded across his bed. He should get up and close the drapes, but he was entirely too lazy. Besides, the sun felt good on his face. He'd missed the sun. It was cold in Alberta this time of year. He thought he'd dream of warm beaches and hot sun. Instead, Nora filled his nighttime thoughts. Erotic dreams. Sweet dreams. Dreams of forever.

He woke up, disoriented in the dark. Sometime while he slept, the sun had gone down. His phone was dead. His body was stiff, but he felt rested. He ambled to the kitchen, stretching as he went. Using the special pods he made in advance; he brewed a cup of half-caf coffee and plugged in his phone. It exploded with messages.

He scanned through them. Work, work, work, Declan, Tom, work. Finally, one from Nora checking in on him. He ignored all the others and punched in her number.

"What?" she asked, her voice heavy with sleep.

"I'm sorry, did I wake you?" He glanced at the time. Four in the morning. Shoot. "I didn't check the time. I just wanted to hear your voice."

"I'm awake now. You do know that it's two a.m. here?" She sounded exhausted, but he heard her smile.

"Sorry about that. I'll check the time before I call again. How was your day?"

"Incredible. I tried those new organic paints on the miniature wood canvases. The results are amazing. I could do a whole series." She talked about her plan for a collection, to be sold as a unit, of twenty-five three by three canvases featuring the sights of Valley Springs. "It's eclectic. It might not sell, but I *need* to paint this."

"Ah, the muse strikes." He chuckled and carried his coffee to the window and stared out at early morning Orlando. From his twenty-fifth-floor suite, he could see for miles. Buildings as far as the eye could see, and further. It was beautiful in its industrial-ness. Nothing like Valley Springs with its quaint houses and trees. He had never longed for anything except city life. He was raised in the small city of Red Deer, Alberta, where his family ran a sporting goods store. Today, he missed the quiet beauty of his brothers' hometown.

"My muse is strong this week." She paused. "I miss you."

Her confession caught him off guard. Primarily because he missed her so badly. "I miss you too, but I won't keep you. Go back to sleep and text me when you're up. I'm heading in to work. I've got a week of vacation to make up for. Can't have them realizing that I can be replaced." He chuckled.

Her answering laugh caught him by surprise, as did her next comment. "That would never do. You'd be fired and have to move in with your brothers."

"That would be tragic." *Or, would it?* "I'll let you go. Get some sleep, babe."

Their Christmas Love

Chapter Nine

Nora sipped her wine. "I'm worried." It had been over a month since she'd seen Ross. "I don't think he's coming back." She sighed. "I mean, he says he coming back. But I don't know if I should believe him."

"You talk for hours almost every night, and your phone is always binging with text messages from him. Trust me," Cyn said, "he's coming back."

"You knew what you were getting into when he left," Eve said. "Long distance isn't easy, especially when you barely know each other. At least he's still calling."

"And texting," Cyn said, her voice heavy with irony. "Always with the texting. Honestly, I don't know how you stand it."

"And I don't know how you can stand not chasing down Declan. You live in the same town and you're not after him like a hound on a fox," Nora said.

"Gross," Eve complained. "How about something less graphic? I'm not a vegan or anything, but that's too vile." She shuddered. "He'll come back."

"Easy for you to say," Nora quipped, "You see Tom once a week, at least."

"I was seeing him. He hasn't asked me to the Winterfest dance. I don't know…" she trailed off sadly. "I mean, I thought we were going. Now I'm not sure."

"Why not?" Nora asked, her heart breaking for her friend who'd been so happy in the past few weeks.

"He's mad because he saw Dexter hug me last week. He won't listen to my explanations. He's totally convinced that Dex has a thing for me. He didn't even give me time to explain that he's my agent and he's gay. Ugh. Men. That's it. I'm going full-on spinster. I'm fifty-three. I don't need a man. I need eight cats."

"Not in my house," Nora laughed. "I just wish Ross had called recently. It's been two days." You know what you should do? You should go to the Winterfest dance. We all should. We'll go as a group and if those idiot brothers show up, good. If not, we move on. There are plenty of fish in the sea."

84

"I tried that dating site and four others. Do you know how rare eligible men our age are? Those that are available have a shipload of baggage. I thought Tom was the one." Eve hugged herself.

"Yeah," Nora sighed. "I thought Ross might be the one."

"I'll never know if Declan is the one." Cyn picked up cookie and shoved the whole thing in her mouth. "Men suck," she declared, showering crumbs everywhere.

"I'm going to that stupid dance, and I'm going to have fun," Nora said. "There have to be other men in this town."

"Yeah, like Ike at the hardware store. He follows you around all the time," Cyn teased.

Nora shuddered. "He's got to be eighty-five. I'm old, but I'm not that desperate."

"Maybe Ross will show up." Eve looked at her watch. "And maybe we should get ready to go. It takes time to become beautiful."

Nora hugged Eve. "You are always beautiful, my friend."

The Winterfest dance was in full swing by the time they arrived half an hour later. Nora scanned the room. Almost everyone was in full costume, including masks. She'd never understand how a winter holiday dance turned into a costume ball. There had to be a hundred and fifty people in the tiny hall. How was she supposed to recognize Ross in this crowd? There were superheroes, princesses, transformers, soldiers, witches, vampires, and everything in between.

Glittering Christmas decorations hung from every available surface. Ceiling, walls, tables. It was a holiday nightmare. There was no color scheme. What happened to sedate red and gold? Or maybe blue and silver? Green and red? Something. The lights were of every conceivable shade, including purple, orange, and nearly black. Obviously, they had reused the decorations from the Halloween party and added some Christmas ones. It looked like the organizers had shopped at garage sales.

"I'm going to get a drink," Cynthia said. "Do I look okay?" She looked down at her toga as if in doubt.

"You look exquisite," Nora said. "And you look great as Wonder Woman too," she said to Eve. They'd

86

spent a long time finding costumes they liked which looked nice on them. Being middle aged didn't mean they couldn't be hot and sexy.

"Thanks," Eve said. "You look exquisite as a mermaid. That tail looks amazing with your curves."

Nora glanced down at herself. "You're sure it's not too much. I mean, I'm fifty-three, hardly a sex siren."

"I beg to differ," Ross said from behind her and swept her into his arms for a kiss. "I nearly had a heart attack when I walked in and saw you." His smile erased all her doubts and sent her pulse through the roof.

"I didn't know you were coming," she said, trying to keep from sounding bitchy. He looked amazing in his Zorro costume. Except for the gray at his temples, he'd pass for a man half his age. The man was sex on a stick. She still wanted to paint him. The hundreds of sketches she'd done since they parted weren't doing anything to dampen that urge.

"I didn't know either. I was supposed to work until the fifteenth. It was a last-minute thing. Our project was delayed due to a parts shortage. I have a few days off. I came in on the red-eye, grabbed a nap, and here I am."

"I'm glad you came." She brushed a kiss across his cheek.

"Not half as glad as I am." He grinned. "We should go."

"What?" Why would he want to leave already? She stared at him, trying to fathom his motives. "Why?"

"Because nobody should see you in that tight mermaid tail but me. Look around, Nora. Every man in the place is starting at you. *ALL* of them from eight to eighty. You're a knockout, and I don't want to them looking at you. Plus, I really, really missed you." His wink was pure seduction.

"Don't be silly. Anticipation is part of the fun." She wrapped her arm around his waist and cuddled in close, his arm around her shoulders. His heat scorched her, filling her with delicious warmth and arousal.

"I've been anticipating being with you for so long that I don't think I can wait any longer. And that outfit? Woman, I want a piece of your tail."

She should have been grossed out by his crude comment. She laughed. "I came here to dance. Let's dance." She tugged him forward. Besides, they needed a stronger foundation for their developing relationship than late night calls and texts and sex. Granted, the sex was incredible. When she was with Ross, she felt young and desirable. That confidence carried over into her day-to-day life. But sex and texts weren't enough to base a relationship on. "Who knows; if you dance well, you might be rewarded later."

"It better be an astronomically good reward. I can't dance." He followed her lead and took her hand. He led her into the classic waltz pose. He smelled delicious. Soap and man. How could the simple combination be so devastating to her sanity?

Beth by Kiss was playing. The melancholy words, wrapped in a slow seductive beat, echoed her feelings when Ross was away. Missing him, wanting to be at his side, unable to go. If it wasn't for the closeness they shared at that moment, she'd have wished for any other song.

"God, I missed you." Ross nuzzled her hair. "You should come stay with me in Florida."

"I can't. I have a daughter to worry about. I'm needed here. You should come home more often." He didn't reply; instead, he swung her into a slow spin away from him and back into his arms. Maybe it was best to drop the subject, at least for the evening. They could enjoy each other's company and worry about details tomorrow. Deep inside, she didn't want to fret over their relationship. Nor did she want to rush him. But part of her needed to know where their relationship was headed. She knew so much about him from their extended phone calls and endless text messages. They seemed compatible, but she didn't know if he was looking for a long-term commitment like she was. He said he was, but did he mean it?

Chapter Ten

Dancing with Nora was bliss. Pure heaven. Ross felt that he'd known her forever. His body remembered every single one of her curves. She was soft and warm in his arms. He wasn't joking when he told her they should leave. He wanted to be alone with her. Naked.

He also knew that spending time in public and with their friends was important. One of his colleagues had lost a girlfriend because he never wanted to go out in public. He wasn't a recluse exactly, he just preferred being at home with her. She had different ideas. Ross didn't want to make that same mistake. Numbers were his thing, people not so much. He was trying to learn by observation.

It would also be a mistake to push the intimacy. Talking on the phone and texting was one thing. Getting to know each other in person was entirely different. He and Nora shared a weird intimacy in their distance communications, and he wasn't sure it would translate in person. Personal confidences felt different when the other person could see your face and read your body language. In person, they felt...he struggled for the word, almost dangerous. Certainly, they were more revealing and awkward. They could hold greater intimacy than sex.

He'd recognized Nora's reluctance to leave immediately. Sure, she'd disagreed and honestly, he was glad she had, even if the other men in the room couldn't keep their eyes off of her. It gave him a primal rush knowing he had the hottest woman in the room. It was chauvinistic and Neanderthal and he knew it, but knowing other men envied him sort of made him the alpha male, the top dog, and he liked it.

"You're thinking very hard," Nora said, glancing up at him.

"I don't mean to be. I'm just distracted by your beauty."

Her laugh sparked a spurt of his own. "I'm giddy because mathematically, there is a one hundred percent chance that you'll come home with me tonight."

She swatted his arm. "Chauvinist. There is a one percent chance."

He faltered. "I was teasing, but just for interest's sake, what do I have to do to amplify the odds? Because, frankly, I've been dreaming of you since I left. I couldn't wait to see you again." It totally sounded like a line, but it was the complete, unvarnished truth.

"Are you serious?" Her expression was somewhere between laughter and bemusement.

"As serious as death and taxes." He spun her in a slow circle. She smelled like Christmas, like orange, and spice, and chocolate. "You smell amazing. I just want to eat you up."

"That's much better than death and taxes." Her smile made him stumble.

"You knock me off balance, just by being with you. Come closer, please." He couldn't stand dancing so far apart. Touching only her hand and her waist wasn't enough. He wanted to feel her full length. She inched forward and with a soft sigh, rested her head on his shoulder. "Much better."

"It is. I like being close to you. Are you here long?"

Why did she have to bring that up? He'd barely arrived and she wanted to know when he was leaving? Bummer.

"Until late Sunday night."

"That's only forty-eight hours!" she exclaimed. "I was hoping you could stay until the New Year."

"In my dreams, Nora, in my dreams. I'll be back on the twentieth. Then, I'm off until January 8th. I can come back to town for part of that. I'll probably spend Christmas with Dec and Tom. My boys won't be home this year. I'll have time to kill."

She stiffened in his arms. What had he said? He reran the conversation in his mind.

"Shit. I didn't mean it that way. You are not just time that I'm killing. You are important to me. That's why I made the long flight just for the weekend. I wanted, needed, to see you. I miss you like crazy, and video calls aren't the same. I need to see your smile in person. Smell your delicious perfume and feel the warmth of your hand in mine. *And her body against his.*

"Well, since you put it that way." She relaxed in his arms.

They danced three slow songs, and when the DJ switched to a faster country song, he led her to the bar for a drink. They sat on stools, watching the crowd.

"Where's Declan? Did he come with you?" She looked around the room. "I saw Tom, or who I assume was Tom. He's Iron Man, right?"

"Tom is Iron Man. He was hoping to dance with your friend, Eve. She makes a great Wonder Woman, but I see that she's dancing with Batman." He sipped his vodka-Pepsi. "Over there," he pointed. "The purple bear, that's Declan dancing with Cynthia."

"They move well together. I wonder if she knows it's him."

"If she doesn't, we shouldn't tell her. I think my shy brother needs to get over himself and learn to talk to women."

"Isn't that kind of mean?" She looked worried.

"Maybe a bit. But it's time for him to realize that not all single women are evil. Take you for example. You're wonderful and kind and sweet."

"Keep it up, Romeo. You might see the inside of my bedroom yet." She winked.

"That isn't my goal," he lied. "I just want to spend time with you. Shall we hit the buffet? Or would you prefer to go out to eat?"

"I think the buffet; I'm not certain this costume is fit for dining out. Although I could become famous as the painter who is dating Zorro. We could really make our mark."

He laughed at the pun on Zorro's trademark and carved an enormous Z in the air with his fake sword. "Buffet it is. Your wish is my command." She took his offered elbow, her hand warm even through his sleeve. He wanted to feel that heat on his skin. He banked the urge and focused on enjoying the moment and the chance to get to know her better.

There was something about Nora that made his heart pound with a dual-edged emotion. Part giddy happiness, part anxiety. Emotions weren't his strong suit. He was a numbers man, not a hearts and flowers guy. Attraction and liking a woman weren't new to him, he'd loved his first wife deeply, but he hadn't felt this way about a woman since she passed away. He was happy, excited, anxious, and totally at peace all at once. He wished he could put the feelings into his calculator or a computer program and make sense of them.

He inhaled slowly and deeply.

"It all smells delicious, doesn't it?" She copied his deep breath.

"It does, and you do too."

"I think you said that already." She chuckled. "But thanks, and I was talking about this incredible buffet." The Legion Ladies had catered the Winterfest dance. Two rows of tables, each eighteen feet long, nearly groaned under the weight of the food. Turkey, chicken, roast beef and pork, potato dishes, salads, pastas, lasagna, casseroles. Perogies, sushi, chow mein, every known vegetable. If you could imagine it, it was on the table. One entire three-foot by six-foot table was devoted to desserts.

"This is a foodie's dream," he declared. "I think I'm in heaven. A delicious beverage, a feast fit for a king, and a beautiful woman on my arm." He paused. "Is that too corny? I hope not because I'm serious. I'm very happy at this moment. Having you here with me doubles my pleasure."

Her cheeks turned an adorable pink. "I'm enjoying myself too. You dance well." She picked up a plate and served herself a bit of roast beef. "Where did you learn to dance?" She had to raise her voice to be heard over *The Macarena*.

"Would you believe high school dance classes?"

"Not for a second. I took those classes. It's hard to learn anything when trying to dance with the high school jocks. They were too busy joking around to put any effort into it."

"I'll have you know that I never danced with the jocks." Her laugh reassured him that she took his comment as the joke he intended. "Or the prom queen for that matter. We danced with who we were assigned by the gym teacher. You're right though. I might have learned a step or two back then, nothing more. My wife and I took dance classes for fun before she became pregnant with the boys."

"Nice. How are the boys?"

"Fabulous. Busy getting their careers underway now that they're honorably discharged from the army. Busy, but content from what I can tell. How is Melissa?"

"Crazy excited about Christmas. She wants a new Play Station, a new phone, and an electric bike. Apparently riding a normal bike is too strenuous. I've already warned her she's not getting the bike. They're crazy expensive, and I want her to understand that Christmas is about love and people. It's for giving, not for getting. It's tough to be the mean parent."

"I can only imagine. I spent a lot of years playing good dad/bad dad. Only I was both parts. We all survived, though at times it was tough. I missed having a wife, but I wouldn't trade the time with my sons for anything."

"That I understand. Totally. Quality time with Melissa is why I followed Dickhead to Valley Springs."

"You never use his name; you just call him Dickhead. Why is that? Is your relationship rough?" He hated the idea that she might be in an uncomfortable situation.

"That's funny. I guess you don't know. Dickhead's name is Richard Headland the Third. What his parents were thinking when they named him, I don't know. He always goes by Richard. But Dickhead seemed to fit once he dumped me. Our relationship is surprisingly good now that we're apart. We make better friends than lovers, I guess. His wife is okay too. She's good with Melissa."

They moved along, filling their plates as they chatted. "I'm glad things are okay." It felt weird talking so seriously about former relationships. "I just realized that this is actually only our second date. Calls and texts aside." He piled turkey and stuffing on his plate, topping them with gravy and green beans. Plates loaded; they found some empty spaces at a round table.

Chapter Eleven

Giddy excitement washed over Nora as Ross walked her to his car. He opened the door for her to get in and paused. He ran a finger down her cheek and looked her in the eyes. "Are you sure?"

Was she sure? Oh, hell yes! She pulled him close for a hot, passionate kiss. She teased his lips apart with her tongue and dove deep for a taste. Mm. Whiskey, chocolate, man. Sweet heaven. "Take me home, Ross. I want to do unspeakable things to you."

"Slow down, we've got all night." He kissed her again. Slowly, deeply, he made love to her mouth. Her knees buckled, and she clutched his shoulders for support.

"Wow," she whispered, unable to draw a full breath. It wasn't just his technique that made her crazy, it was something about the man himself. It was like her soul knew his. It didn't make sense, but that's how it felt deep in her heart.

He kissed her cheek. "I'll take that as a compliment." He flashed a rakish grin and helped her into the car. She let him buckle her seatbelt and stole another kiss as he leaned over her. She shivered with anticipation. Would tonight be as devastatingly knee buckling as the last time? Part of her was certain the sexual chemistry they shared was a fluke and that they'd never be able to repeat that magic.

He climbed in and pulled out of the parking lot. They had remote started the car, so it was nice and toasty. She unbuttoned her wool jacket and leaned back against the headrest to look out the window. Enormous snowflakes drifted down, swirling in front of the headlights as they drove down Main Street. Businesses were lit with holiday lights, their window displays showing the best holiday gifts. It was magical and not just because of the electricity sparking between her and Ross.

"It's beautiful along here. I adore the lights. There's just something about them that gives me a happy glow." It was deeper than that, but hard to express. The lights reminded her to be kinder and more generous. The drifting snow spoke of the warmth she felt in her heart for her friends and family. She sighed happily; she loved this time of year. That feeling, in a nutshell, was why she kept Christmas lights up in her studio. Sometimes, late at night, she'd work in the dark with only the glow of tiny colored LED bulbs to illuminate her creative vision.

"It is pretty," he agreed, dragging her mind back to the vehicle and the present. "Will I get to see your paintings?" He waggled his eyebrows.

She hesitated. Her work was private, until it was finished. She didn't like to show off incomplete work. It had taken years before she'd showed her roommates incomplete works. Ross was still a stranger, and she was reluctant to share. Especially not the current trend of sketching him. She was getting better in the past month and a half, but didn't feel ready to expose her growing abilities. Logically, she was pretty good, better than most, but she had a reputation, and her own personal standards to live up to.

"It's okay if you're not comfortable. I know creative types can be weird that way. I didn't even know Declan was the author of one of my favorite series. How could I not know that?" His voice carried a hint of anger, despite his light laugh. "Tom's different. If he can convince you to haul wood or do manual labor, you're welcome in his workshop anytime. Where do you fall?" With his eyes on the road, and one hand on the steering wheel, he grasped her left hand in his right.

It was a good question, and not at all judgmental. "Secretive, I guess. At least until the work is finished. I've turned down several offers to teach beginner art classes because I'm not good with sharing my work in the early stages. I feel bad, it could be inspiring for new artists." She shrugged. "But, play your cards right and you might get a limited showing. Maybe." She tried not to sound hesitant.

"No pressure, Nora. I understand. We're in the early stages of friendship, and revealing your muse is a big step." He raised her hand to his lips and kissed her palm.

Shivers raced over her skin, arousal re-bloomed, and her nerve endings sparked to life. At least half of her excitement was because he was patient with her creative shyness. She squeezed his hand. "Drive faster." His chuckle warmed her through.

Five minutes later, they dashed through the swirling snow and into the house.

"Would you like a drink? I bought some fifteen-year-old Scotch." She twisted her hands together behind her back. The short run into the house had reignited her nerves. She wasn't accustomed to seducing men. She wanted Ross. Badly. Despite sharing herself with him during his last visit, she was experiencing a sudden attack of nerves.

Would he find her stretch marks repulsive? What about her less than perky breasts? Would she be able to please him again, or was last time a fluke? She wanted to bang her head into the wall. Where was all this insecurity coming from? She was a mature, confident woman, not a twittering virgin.

Ross looked at her. He tilted his head left, then right, and his brows pinched together for a fraction of a second. "Come here, beautiful. I need to kiss you."

She took three steps toward him and paused. She clenched her hands until her nails bit into her palms. What was wrong with her?

"Shy?" he whispered. He took two small steps until they were almost touching. "Nora Ravine, you are the most beautiful woman I know. Just being with you leaves me breathless. My heart pounds when you are close. Feel." He slid his hand down her arm and pulled her hand from behind her back. He opened her fingers, one by one, and placed her hand on his heart.

It pounded under her touch. *She did that to him? Unbelievable.*

"I can see your pulse pounding too. Here," he touched her wrist, "and here." He traced a finger along her jaw. Prickles of anticipation ran down her spine. He looked thoughtful. "If you're nervous, or scared, or you've changed your mind, I can go. Or we can have a drink and relax. The next move is yours, beautiful lady."

Her heart melted. She hadn't said a word, yet he'd known she was tense. It took a special man to notice, and to care, that she was uncertain.

"Let's try that Scotch." He pulled her other hand forward and held both her hands between his. "One drink, and then I'll go." He didn't sound upset or disappointed.

She didn't try to stop the slow smile curving up the corners of her mouth.

"That's better. You have a beautiful smile."

"Screw the drink." She pulled one hand free of his and using the other, led him upstairs. Unable to help herself, she paused at the doorway to Melissa's room, just to be certain she hadn't come home. At thirteen, sometimes it was a treat to stay alone even if her father was just next door.

"Thank God, she's not here. I don't think I could have…never mind." She forced a laugh and tugged him down the hall to the master suite.

Standing beside the four-poster bed, she knew another moment of anxiety and trepidation. Ross cupped her face in his hands and whispered, "I've waited years for you." He brushed his lips across hers and nibbled her lower lip.

Tension flooded from her shoulders and lodged low in her belly as arousal bloomed under his tender attention. Her skin prickled with a hot chill of lust. The hair on the back of her neck stood up in aroused anticipation.

"Come lie down with me. I need to be beside you." His soft words brushed across her ear like a whisper soft caress.

Awkwardly, she hitched her mermaid tail to the side, climbed onto the bed and lay down facing him, head propped up on her elbow. Standing at the edge, his gaze tangled with hers, he unbuckled his belt to remove his sword. "Hey, eyes are up here," he teased when she glanced lower.

Laughing, she got to her knees and crawled her way back to him. "Come here." She flicked open the first button on his black shirt. One after another she released them until his entire chest was revealed. She slid her hands under the silky fabric to caress his firm muscles. He must work out because, damn, he was hot and hard. She stroked the downy hairs on his chest; they weren't as long as she recalled. "Did you trim your chest hair?"

"Always. Manscaping is important." He groaned when her fingers brushed his nipples. "You caught me unprepared last time."

"I like it." She fluttered kisses across his pecs. He groaned. She pushed the shirt off his shoulders; it slid down his arms and held fast at the wrists. He wiggled, trying to free himself.

"Shoot. I'm stuck." He inched back from her and struggled with the shirt.

"Are you saying I can do whatever I want?"

"Help me out of this, please."

"Hmm." She tapped her lips and grinned. "Maybe in a bit. I have exploring to do." She licked and kissed her way down his abdomen. He tasted so good. Salty, musky, almost a bit sweet.

"Nora," he groaned. "You're going to pay for this." His exasperation made her laugh. She kissed some more, trailing her lips along the top of his pants as she fiddled with the button closure.

He could have freed himself from the shirt if he wanted to. He wasn't stuck that badly, yet he played along. It was heady and empowering that such a strong virile man would set aside his strength to play with a woman. And this *was* play, of the best sort.

She couldn't stop the grin that formed as she pulled his zipper down with her teeth. His agonized groan went straight to the center of her core. And maybe, just a little, to her heart.

Their Christmas Love

Chapter Twelve

Texting sucked. Ross stared at his phone. He'd had a fabulous time with Nora. They'd spent every minute of the weekend together. He'd been annoyed when he had to leave. He wasn't ready to part from her. They texted and talked over and over, all month long. It wasn't enough, but he was busy with work and couldn't get away.

Time passed way too slowly and at the same time sped by with his long work hours. Before he knew it, it was December twenty-third, and Ross was on his way back to Valley Springs to spend Christmas with his brothers and with Nora. He had hoped to arrive sooner, but a few glitches delayed his portion of the project, and he couldn't leave until it was finished.

Nora had seemed understanding when he called, but he had his doubts. He watched a number of coworkers along with his brother Tom struggle with relationships when they were deep into work. For Tom, it was the creative zone, not unlike Nora's. For his coworkers, it was the fluctuating demands of their jobs. They did their nine-to-five, but when required, they put in the extra hours, sacrificing their personal lives.

This was why men died earlier than women. They gave everything to their jobs. The women he worked with had better work/life balances. If he was going to pursue anything serious with Nora, he was going to have to work on his own balance. He'd let the younger, single men take the long shifts. He'd use up years of back vacation and spend more time in Alberta.

Instead of going Declan's, Ross drove his rental car directly to Nora's. Just as he pulled into the driveway, Nora and Eve exploded out of the front door laughing. His breath caught in his throat at the sight of Nora's beautiful smile. She was breathtaking. Her hair flowed down her back in a sheet of glistening waves. Her wool jacket was unbuttoned showing off a lacy blouse and blue jeans. She had on the sexiest black boots that came up over her knees. Instantly, he could picture her wearing those boots and nothing else. He was rock hard in an instant. His pulse thundered even as a sense of peace stole over him.

"Ladies," he greeted them.

They stopped dead. Half a second later, Nora raced down the sidewalk and flung herself into his arms. "Ross! I'm glad you're back."

She kissed him with such passion, he completely forgot where they were. Her warm welcome settled something in his heart he hadn't realized was jumpy. "Wow! That's some welcome." He kissed her again, this time with less passion and more caring. "Where are you ladies off to?"

"Anywhere but here," Nora exclaimed. "Declan and Cynthia are in there. They just made up after a massive fight. Now they're all kissy faced." She laughed. "We thought it best to leave them alone. We're going to the pub for a few drinks and a bit to eat. Why don't you join us?"

"I think I will." He wrapped his arm around her waist and walked her toward his car. "We'll take my car, unless you object. It's already warm." He shivered. "I'd forgotten how cold it is here, even with the down jacket."

They chatted about the weather until they reached the pub. Settled in with drinks and appetizers, Nora launched into a reciting of the issues that had nearly torn Declan and Cynthia apart.

He wished he could have been here for his brother in his time of stress, but he was at least partially relieved to have missed it all. Ninety minutes later, they were joined by Declan, Cynthia, and Tom.

Tom took one look at Eve and stomped out. Something was up between them. He'd have to talk to Tom once they got home. He winced internally. If he went home to talk to Tom, he wouldn't be able to spend the night with Nora. Crap.

At midnight, Ross found Tom drunk on the stairwell at home. He was struggling to put his boots on. "Dude, you can't possibly be this drunk."

"Yeah. I'm not. I just want to go outside and freeze my ass off. Leave me be." He snorted out a raw laugh. "Women."

"Boy, that says a lot. What did you do?" Ross asked, shedding his jacket and hanging it up before kicking off his hiking boots.

Tom dropped his boots on the mat and flopped onto the sofa with his jacket still on. "What makes you think I did something? Maybe she did something. Did you ever consider that? No, you just immediately took her side."

"Want to talk about it?" He wandered to the fireplace and struck a match to light the logs already laid out and waiting. "Why don't I pour us a drink?" Lord knows he needed one, though Tom definitely did not. He'd been planning on spending the night with Nora and she'd shooed him away so she could be there for Eve, since Declan and Cynthia were wrapped up in post-fight bliss. Some Christmas this was turning out to be. It was a darned good thing there were a couple days until they were all supposed to get together for Christmas Day dinner.

"Scotch for me," Tom said. "There's a bottle of Jura there someplace."

"I don't know how you drink that stuff. It's too smoky for me." He rummaged in the liquor cabinet and unearthed a bottle of Old Pulteney. He grabbed glasses, a bucket of ice, some cold water, and the two bottles and loaded them on a cookie sheet. He carried them to the living room and poured them each a drink.

"To women," he toasted.

"May they rot in hell," Tom countered bitterly and downed his drink in one shot.

"May they make us more human," Ross said. He took a small sip, taking a moment to enjoy the rich flavors. He crossed the room and lit the tree. "That's better. We need some holiday spirit." He lit a couple candles in snowman holders on the coffee table. They must be Cynthia's touch; Dec didn't go for many knickknacks.

He sat across from Tom. "So, what happened?" His brother poured another drink and slammed it back. It was going to be a long night if this kept up.

"She skipped three dates. Three!" He sneered. "She forgot." He put air quotes around forgot. "She was making some stupid sculpture and says she lost track of time."

"Maybe she did. I can get wrapped up in a math problem for days. I know Nora goes off and paints for hours at a time and forgets to call or text. Hell, you get wrapped up in carving as well. You only quit when varnish needs to dry or you can't hold a chisel in your aching hands. Give the woman a break." He paused. "Or is there something else?"

Knowing Tom's slow thinking habits, Ross went to the kitchen and found some chips and dip. He grabbed them, a sharp knife, and a roll of garlic sausage. He sat on the far end of the couch and carved off a chunk of meat. He passed it to Tom.

"What?" He knew his brother would hear the wealth of questions in the single word. Brevity could be a good thing.

"I saw her kissing some guy. She's probably dating us both."

Ross considered the statement. "Eve? Seeing two guys at once? She doesn't seem the type. You must have misunderstood. Explain what you saw."

"They were outside the post office. He had his arms around her. She hugged him tight and kissed him."

"Are we talking peck on the cheek, or tongue down his throat?" he asked logically.

"Fine. It was a peck." His voice was heavy with pain and accusation.

"And you went right up to them and introduced yourself to him, right?"

117

"No." Tom slammed back another drink. When had his brother developed this type of tolerance to alcohol?

"Did you ask her about it?" Ross moved the bottles out of easy reach.

"No. Why would I? If she wants some other guy, she's welcome to him. I just want her to be happy."

"She didn't seem happy tonight. She seemed as miserable as you. Why don't you talk to her? Ask her about him? What can it hurt? I mean, besides your pride? Who knows, maybe you misunderstood and you can go back to dating. I know how much you like her." He spent hours on the phone with his brothers every week. He knew that Tom loved Eve. He just had to get off his stubborn ass and fix the mess between them.

His phone vibrated in his pocket. He pulled it out. Nora. Wishing him a good night.

Ross: Sweet dreams. I'll see you tomorrow.

He hit send.

Ross: Hey, Tom's pissed. He saw Eve kissing some guy, what's up with that?

Nora: That's Dexter. He's her agent. She just landed a big contract for sculptures using old oilfield parts. She'll have pieces in oilfield offices all over the province and in the museum. Oh no! Ross got the wrong idea?

Ross: He did. He knee-jerk reacted. Thanks for the heads up. Maybe I can mitigate the damages. Sleep well, sweetheart.

Sweetheart? Where had that come from?

He tucked his phone away and hid his smile. No sense making Tom even more miserable. "Maybe the guy was someone she works with?" He threw the idea out, trying to make it seem like a random thought. "You know, maybe another artist or shop owner."

"She was all over him." Tom grabbed the chips and started eating, double dipping them.

Gross. Ross made a mental note to pitch the dip in the trash when his brother was finished. "I think you should ask her. Give her a chance to explain. Maybe it was a cousin, her lawyer." He snapped his finger. "Does she have an agent?"

"How the hell would I know? But ya, I think so."

"You've been dating her for three months. Don't you talk?"

Tom grinned sadly. "Yeah, but mostly we…"

"Don't go there. Seriously? You're this broken up about a bed bunny?" He was provoking Tom on purpose. He'd get his hackles up and maybe the light would dawn.

"She's not a damned bed bunny. She's a beautiful, intelligent woman. She's talented, hot as hell in bed." He glared. "And don't even think about her that way or I'll kick your ass. She's perfect. She's so kind and sweet. She's happy and loving."

"Except the missed dates and the other guys." He poked again. Either his brother would see the light or Ross would take a fist to the guts.

"Maybe she had a reason. I dunno. If it was just one, I could get over it, but there was Batman at the dance too."

"Call her. Text her. Ask her."

"No." He frowned. "I tried before. She refused to answer calls or texts." His words were starting to slur badly. There wasn't much time to get him to see the light before he passed out.

"Bro, it's less than thirty hours until Christmas. I kind of had the impression you were going to propose. What happened to that plan? You sure can't propose if you're having a hissy fit over a little necking."

"Shut the hell up." Tom bounced to his feet seeming way too sober for someone who'd downed several shots since arriving home. He towered over Ross, glaring.

Ross bit back a grin and held up his hands in surrender. "Think about it. Maybe you made a mistake. Maybe she did. But if you don't talk about it, you'll never know. Get some sleep, Tom." He rose and patted his brother on the back. "I'm going to bed. I've got a breakfast date."

He walked from the room and came back again.

"Remember, she's like you, and Dec, and Cyn, and Nora…creative as hell. The creative mind is weird. It works differently. Maybe you can get past her tendency to be late and her kissing strange men. Work something out." He took the Scotch with him when he left.

Chapter Thirteen

Nora sat with Cynthia and watched Eve pace the living room, glass of wine in her hand. "Slow down, before you spill that. The rug is beige, in case you hadn't noticed. Red wine will stain." She couldn't care less about the carpet in the face of her friend's broken heart, but over the long years of their friendship, she'd learned that distraction was a good way to get Eve thinking.

"Right. Sorry." She set the glass down and resumed pacing. The grandfather clock in the corner chimed two. "Holy crap. It's Christmas Eve morning."

"Yup." What else could she say? "Try and unwind. Maybe get some sleep. Things always look brighter in the morning."

"Seriously? Platitudes? Where's the actual advice? Give me something to work with before I stomp over there and kick his stupid backside."

"Shouldn't you be more Zen, you know, being a yoga instructor? Chill. Do some downward facing cow or that thing where you lay flat on your back and breathe, you know dead man's float."

"Downward face dog, down-dog for the kids. And that last one is corpse pose. And no, they wouldn't help. I'm too worked up. I really thought he'd soften. If I'd known he was going to show up, I'd have stayed home."

Me too! Nora didn't voice the thought. She'd been super excited when Ross arrived a full day early. Dinner and drinks could have been fun. Dec and Cyn were totally hyped up and in love. Engaged, she could hardly believe it. But Tom's sighs and Eve's sad looks put a damper on the party.

She could be cuddled up in bed with Ross right now. Making love, talking until the wee hours. Instead, she was here, consoling her friend. Or at least trying to get her to see reason. She'd texted him that she was going to bed, just to see if he'd chat. Apparently not. He was in the same dilemma as she was. She pulled out her phone.

Nora: Maybe we can trick them into getting together.

Ross: I thought you went to bed.

Nora: I wish! Just trying to talk Eve in off the ledge.

Ross: What are you thinking?

Nora: Trick them into coming to the same place. Lock them in until they talk.

Ross: Know any good places?

Nora: No.

Nora: Oh, wait. The library has an old book room. You have to be buzzed in and out by staff, unless you know the code. Maybe Cyn will help.

Ross: You get her to the library; I'll get him there.

Nora: Crap. Library is closed. I'll talk to Cyn in the morning…maybe she'll help.

Ross: Ok. Now, I'm really going to bed. Sweet dreams.

Nora: Good night. (Kiss emoji)

"Ugh. You're sick. It's the middle of the night and you're all smiley and kissy faced while you text your boyfriend," Eve sneered.

"Yup. Our relationship isn't without issues, but at least we talk." *When they weren't burning up the sheets.* "Look, I think you should talk to him. Maybe you won't make up, but at least if you talk to him, you'll know he heard your side. Does he even know you have an agent? How much of your past does he know?"

"All of it. Every sordid detail." She sighed. "But I never thought to mention Dexter. I rarely talk to him. Most of my work comes through my website now. I sure wasn't expecting that commission. I was so excited."

"You should be, and you should be proud. If Tom can't see that, maybe you should ditch him for good. But not until you talk to him."

"I'll think about it." She refilled her wine. "I'm going to have a hot bath. Good night."

"Good night."

"I'm out too," Cynthia said. "Declan's waiting. Buck up, Eve. Things will look better soon."

"Shut out the lights when you go to bed." Eve walked away leaving Nora alone in the living room.

Nora cleared away the wine and their cake plates. Leaving the tree lit, she threw a couple logs and a bundle of dried orange slices into the fire. She settled on the couch to watch the fire glowing in the fireplace. The sweet scent of orange and cinnamon filled the air. Next year, she'd add a few cloves to those fire bundles.

"Whatever happened to good will toward man?" she asked the room. "Love conquers all, and all that stuff." She sighed and cuddled under a red and white fleece throw. "Merry Christmas, Nora."

She wished she could sneak over to see Ross, but he'd gone to bed for the night. She consoled herself with the knowledge that seeing him tonight had been a bonus since he wasn't due until tomorrow.

Their Christmas Love

Chapter Fourteen

Nora stood in the kitchen on Christmas morning, watching light fluffy flakes of snow fall through the early morning darkness. Nobody was awake except her. This was her favorite time of the year. This exact moment. The breakfast muffins were cooked. The cinnamon buns were cooling, and the ham and cheese quiche was already in the oven. By the time everyone else was awake, breakfast would be ready. She loved the last few days before Christmas.

Melissa was past believing in Santa, but every year, he came anyway. Late after everyone went to sleep, Nora crept out of bed, filled the stockings, and slid extra gifts under the tree. Nothing big, just little things to let everyone know she cared. Melissa would eat breakfast while they opened gifts, then she'd go to her father's for the day. She'd return, with her father and his new family, for Christmas dinner. It was a tradition they'd started at Melissa's request.

129

Sometimes it was awkward, usually it went okay. This year would be different. Ross and his brothers would be joining them for the day. She could hardly wait for them to arrive. It was so perfectly in keeping with the miracle of Christmas that both her best friends were engaged to the men they loved, and brothers at that.

She walked through the living room to ensure that everything was perfect. Not that it would have changed since last night, but she wanted perfection for her first Christmas with Ross.

The stockings were hung perfectly. One for each of the six adults and one for Melissa. Her ex would do gifts at his place later on. Still, she'd sent him and his family a small gift because they were so great with Melissa. Upstairs, someone started moving. She rubbed her hands together. Today would be perfect.

Eight hours later, she snuggled into Ross's side on the couch. He had loved the little book she'd found him called *Avogadro's Number*. It was a pocket guide with a collection of mathematical formulas. A bit dated with today's computers and calculators, but what else did you get a guy you were falling for but still didn't know very well? "This was the best day ever." She sighed happily. "Thanks again for the paints and for sharing Christmas with us."

"I can't believe that your plan worked." Ross's laugh rumbled through her. "Eve and Tom locked in the library for three hours, and they actually talked."

"I can't believe he proposed to her."

"And she accepted. We're practically family now," she said, half joking. Wouldn't it be amazing if she and Ross became engaged? Not that she'd ask him. There were too many unresolved questions between them, and they still didn't really know each other.

Would he retire and move back to Valley Springs, or maybe get a job here? Could she move there? She couldn't picture leaving her daughter, but for the right man, she might consider it. She nearly laughed aloud. *Liar. You're wouldn't leave Melissa for anyone. At least not before she starts college. You're her mom. She needs you.*

"What have you got planned for the new year?" she asked.

"I think I might be up for a promotion at work." His voice rang with pride. "I'm hoping I get it. It will mean a big pay jump and more responsibilities."

"Oh? I thought you might be thinking about retiring." He had mentioned the idea in passing, and she wondered if he'd changed his mind.

"I probably could, but I'd like to build up my nest egg a bit." There was something in his voice she couldn't identify. Fear? Dishonesty? Doubt?

"Oh." She struggled for something to say. "I guess I'm lucky. My nest egg is fine, and I can putter with my art until I'm old and gray, well, grayer." She had more than a few gray strands. They didn't bother her. There were badges of honor from all she'd been through.

"I'll have to look into hobbies before I retire. You know, something to do when I don't have to go to work anymore."

"Hobbies?" Anger flared up her spine. "You think my art is a hobby?" Who did he think he was? "I can't believe you said that. How dare you?"

"I didn't say that. You're twisting my words. I said I wanted to have something to do when I retire. Don't get all bent out of shape over nothing. You're being overly sensitive."

"And you're being an ass." She took a deep breath and confessed her feelings. "I thought maybe you'd retire soon, move to Valley Springs, and spend your free time with me. We could travel and spend our retirement together."

"Sure, that sounds great." Sarcasm dripped from his voice. "Maybe I could be your houseboy. Do the cooking and cleaning while you get rich from your art. That sounds perfect."

She pushed out of his arms and jumped to her feet. "Are you saying you have no interest in a future with me? I get it, we haven't been seeing each other for long, but if I'm only around for casual sex when you stumble back to town, I'm not interested. I'm too old to waste my time on a man who isn't interested in a future."

He started to speak, but she was irate and refused to let him get a word in edgewise. She held up her hand in a stop motion.

"Zip it! I'm not finished. I'm not asking you to lock anything down or promise me forever. I just need to know where you see this relationship going. Am I just a fling? Do you see a future? No need to map that future out, I just need to know if it is possible. Can you ever retire and move closer to me? I have a child, and I'll be here until she starts university. She was a late baby, we tried for years before we were blessed with Melissa. I'm not leaving her. I'm retiring right here in Valley Springs, and I will never, ever stop painting."

"Stop overreacting." The placating tone in his voice was like throwing gas on the fires of her anger.

"Overreacting?" She glared and literally saw red through her squinted eyes. "Know this, Ross Foxx. I. Am. Not. Over. Reacting. But I am one hundred percent serious. If you aren't in this relationship for a possible future, you can get the hell out of my house."

"What if I don't know what I want?" He crossed his arms over his chest.

Her stomach dropped to her knees. Butterflies stampeded in her belly. She blinked back tears. No! She wouldn't cry. Not in front of him. "I'll tell you what," she said calmly. "Why don't you go back to Florida and when you figure out what you want from life, give me a call?"

"You're kicking me out? Be reasonable. Can't we discuss this?"

She clenched her fists so she wouldn't punch him.

"Yes, we can discuss this. After you know what you want from life. You're fifty-four years old, Ross. Don't you think it's time you figured your shit out?" She backed away from the couch and made a move-along gesture toward the door. "Figure it out, and if there's a place for me, let me know. But know this, I'm not going to sit at home knitting, waiting for your call."

He stood and came close to her. She wouldn't give him the satisfaction of backing away; she held her ground. She managed not to flinch when he reached out and stroked her cheek.

"Don't be hasty, Nora. Don't throw me out of your life."

"I'm not. I'm telling you to get a damned plan. Once you do, I'll welcome a call. Have a nice life." She walked to the front door and stood there waiting.

Frowning, he pulled on his jacket and boots. She expected another weak objection. Silently, he looked at her, a sad look in his beautiful dark brown eyes. He pulled on his gloves. He leaned forward and brushed a kiss across her lips. "I'm sorry." He opened the door and walked out into the falling snow.

She closed the inside door and pressed her back against it. Slowly, she slid to the floor. This was the worst Christmas ever.

Cyn and Dec were at his place, together.

Eve and Tom were upstairs, together.

Melissa was at her father's.

Nora was alone. Brutally, painfully alone. She buried her head in her hands and let the tears fall. Part of her knew that caring for someone, maybe even loving someone, was never a mistake, but unrequited love sucked.

Chapter Fifteen

For weeks, he avoided his brothers' calls and texts. Their happiness ate at his heart and soul. He was jealous of their happiness, plain and simple. He wanted what they had, and he hated his inability to celebrate their good fortune. His mind turned to Nora. God, he missed her. His heart ached like a broken tooth. He'd never felt pain like this. Ever. It was worse than when he'd broken his leg crashing his dirt bike when he was twenty.

Every fiber of his being wanted to call her or text her. He hurt with need to talk to her.

He couldn't, because for the life of him, he didn't know what he wanted out of life. She'd been brutally right; he had no idea where his life was going and had been totally oblivious to his own unseeable future.

He liked Nora. A lot. But he wasn't ready to pack up his life, his career, everything on the off chance that he could build a relationship with her. If he knew what he'd do in Valley Springs, it might make a difference. But no future and an unstable relationship wasn't something he could give up his current life for. He needed...certainty.

Late in February, his phone beeped, breaking his concentration on double checking some calculations for the next shuttle launch.

Declan. He read the text message, he had read them all and listened to all the messages. Every single one of them. Both his brothers texted at least five or six times every day since he'd left town the day after Christmas. More than one message chided him for not saying goodbye to everyone.

Declan: We need you to check some numbers for us. Please.

Dirty pool, playing on his love of math.

Ross: What numbers?

Declan: For the business. We're planning on opening an art gallery here in Valley Springs. You'd know that if you read your emails. You don't answer messages or calls, so we assume you don't want to buy in, but we'd like you to double check what we've got before we commit ourselves and sign the lease. Please.

How could he turn them down? He didn't want them to enter into a risky venture, even if he wasn't part of it.

Ross: Fine. Send them to me. I'll look after work tonight.

Declan: Best brother ever!

He wished he lived up to the praise. He wasn't much of a brother. They'd been texting all month about their business plan. Part of him wished he had the guts to return to Valley Springs and be a partner. He was already dreading the summer. Declan and Cynthia and Tom and Eve were having a double wedding the first weekend in June. There was no way he could avoid going. Neither brother had asked him yet, but he knew he'd be asked to be their best man. And he'd say yes.

Curious about the numbers, he started looking at them immediately. The business plan was solid. They'd done top-notch research on demographics, potential artists to invite, expenses, revenue, utilities. They'd covered literally everything. The numbers added up, and they stood to make a lot of money. They had verbal agreements with fifteen artists, including Nora and Eve who would be full partners. They'd decided on a large two-story building on Main Street and an empty warehouse in Valley Springs' small industrial area. They'd rent stalls in the warehouse to artists who needed workspace.

He flipped to the last pages. It was a formal letter inviting him to become partner. The buy in was small, practically miniscule. The letter also invited him to join them as manager with a small salary which would ratchet up with sales.

He stared at the page, reading it over and over. Excitement built low in his belly and grew until his entire body felt giddy. This could be the semi-retirement he needed!

He was going to do this. He signed the agreement. Only he wouldn't mail it back; he'd deliver it in person. He had two months of vacation stacked up and was being told to use it or lose it.

Decision made, he felt lighter, freer, than he had in years. He typed up his notice and delivered it to his boss and apologized for leaving with no notice. "I've got vacation due, and I'd already booked the next two weeks off. You'll find someone to replace me." There was an up-

and-coming junior mathematician who had all they skills they'd need. Ross gave him a solid referral and packed up his desk.

Three days later, his apartment was empty and up for sale, and he was boarding a plane to Canada. The moving company would store his belongings until he found a place to live. Giddiness washed over him. He felt like a kid again. He hadn't had this much energy or felt this kind of excitement since…if he were honest, he'd say since he met Nora. Instead, he pushed that idea away and said since he was a kid.

Try though he might, he couldn't stop thinking about Nora and how great it felt to know they could spend more time together without feeling rushed into something long-term.

♥♥♥

Before he knew what hit him, he was up to his elbows in paint and spending his free time looking at office furniture and flooring. There was an easy camaraderie with his brothers and a nagging sense that he should contact Nora, but he didn't want to rush things. Okay, he was scared to call her.

He was edging the gallery walls in preparation for their final coat of paint when the small bells on the front door chimed. "You better have coffee," he called out, expecting one of his brothers.

"And donuts," a soft female voice responded. "I heard you like crullers."

Nora.

The paintbrush clattered to the floor. "Shoot." He climbed down off the ladder, careful not to trip in his haste to see her again. "Nora. Hi." He barely pushed the words past the excitement clogging his throat.

"Ross, good to see you." Her smile didn't reach her eyes, and her voice had a hard edge.

He probably should have called her when he got back to town. He had wanted to see her again, but hadn't wanted to rush into a relationship. No, he wouldn't lie to himself. He'd been ashamed of his actions at Christmas and hadn't had the guts to face her. In her place, he'd be annoyed.

Well, if she could try her best to be civil, he would too. He'd avoid the temptation to rush over and kiss her senseless. She looked beautiful in her paint-stained sweat

142

pants and baggy T-shirt. Her hair was caught up in some kind of paint spattered cloth. Random tendrils poked out here and there. He banked the urge to reach out and smooth them. She looked exhausted. God, she was beautiful.

"Give me a second to wrap up this brush so it doesn't dry out." *And to calm his thundering pulse and control the rush of testosterone washing over him because she was within touching distance.* "Take a seat. I'll be right there." His fingers trembled as he covered the brush in kitchen wrap and hammered the lid onto the paint can. He took several deep breaths before joining her.

"Thanks for the coffee." He sat across from her at the small folding table that served as a snack table and workspace.

"You look nice."

She laughed wryly. "You should get your glasses checked. I'm a wreck." She blushed.

"To me, you are lovely. Paint spatters and all. You wear them much better than I do." He winked without meaning to.

"You are a mess." She laughed at his paint-stained clothing. "You haven't even done one wall, and you've got splatters everywhere. It's a good thing the new floors don't go in until the painting is finished."

"Yeah, I'm not good with my hands," he said.

She blushed again. Oh-ho where had her mind gone? Maybe there was still hope of winning her over.

"Give me numbers and I'm a happy man. Paint, not so much." *Okay, all he really needed was her, in the same place he was.* He battled the urge to touch her, or kiss her, or push her up against the wall and— He slammed the brakes on that idea.

"That makes us opposites. I hate numbers. I have an accountant for a reason. But paint? Paint is heaven. Even painting walls. Want some help?"

"Yes! Please! This place is huge. We decided to paint it ourselves to save money. But when I agreed, I didn't realize *we* meant *me*." He chuckled.

"Give me a tour? I haven't had the chance to look around yet. I wasn't there when your brothers chose the building."

"Sure." He stood, cruller in one hand, coffee in the other. "This is the main showroom." He waved his donut around the large space. "We've had the windows treated to block UV light. We don't want to fade any artwork. We have a guy coming in tomorrow to add a glass foyer. Something to trap a bit of warm air when the outer door opens in winter."

To the left of the main room were two smaller, brightly lit but windowless galleries.

"These will be used for showcasing Indigenous Canadian art and pieces from other cultures. The world has so much multicultural talent, we want to showcase a variety."

"Somehow, I didn't expect you to know much about art."

He knew she didn't mean the comment as a slight or insult. "Honestly, I don't. But I'm learning fast. I'm taking an online class in art appreciation. I'll be responsible for the day-to-day operations, but you, Eve, and Tom will be in charge of finding suitable artists." There was a small staff room in the back and two more small display rooms.

"I knew this place was large, but I had no idea. It seems bigger on the inside."

"I was surprised too." His fingers itched to pull her closer. He wanted nothing more than to kiss her senseless.

Chapter Sixteen

They painted all day in companionable silence. Nora wondered what was going on in Ross's mind. He kept smiling at her and every time he did, her pulse thundered in her ears. It was approaching suppertime when they finished the final coat.

"I'm starving," she said.

"Me too." He looked around the gallery. "This place looks great though. We work well together." He paused and fiddled with a screwdriver on the table before looking up at her. "Can I buy you dinner?"

"Dinner?"

"You know, that final meal of the day. Meat, potatoes, dessert, and some wine? Most people indulge."

His teasing wink went straight to her heart. It was so good to see him again. They hadn't talked since he bolted at Christmas. Maybe they could try again. "You know what? Dinner would be nice. Can I change first?"

147

"Sure. I'll pick you up in an hour. Maybe we can try that new place outside of town on Oak Street. What's it called again?"

"Tamarack; the chef came out here on vacation last spring. I guess he liked it because, according to gossip, he left a high paying job in Calgary to open his own restaurant. The food is supposed to be exquisite, even if he's a bit temperamental with people." She smiled at Ross. Tamarack was supposed to be intimate and romantic. Did he know that? If not, she wasn't going to mention it. "I can be ready in an hour. See you then."

They locked up and walked out together. "Later," Ross said as she climbed into her car.

♥♥♥

Ross cleaned up in record time. Ten minutes after he was home, he was showered and shaved. He debated his clothing for entirely too long before settling on a sport coat and dress pants. No tie. This was a date between...what were they exactly? Business partners, friends, lovers, ex-lovers? Soon to be family?

"I don't give a shit. It's dinner with a beautiful woman, and I enjoy her company. That's all that matters."

"Talking to yourself, Ross?" Tom leaned against the bedroom doorjamb. When would he learn to shut the door before he showered? He kept forgetting he shared a house with his brothers and didn't live alone in a Florida condo.

"Actually, yes."

"Nervous?"

"Hell yes!" There was no shame in admitting that he was apprehensive and excited over this date. His brothers knew how badly breaking up with Nora had hurt. He was going to be on his best behavior this time. He didn't want to screw this up.

"Go easy, okay? You hurt Nora badly. She went weeks without painting. That's not good. You nearly killed her muse. Besides, if you mess this up, Eve will have my ass. If that happens, I'll kick yours. Capisce?"

"Yeah, yeah. I understand. I need to go easy. My goal is to start over from scratch. I'm here, she's here. I'm semi-retired. I think there's a chance we can make this work. If we're compatible. I promise, no shenanigans."

"Utmost respect and honesty?" Declan added as he walked in.

"Is there no privacy in this house?" he asked, knowing there wasn't.

"Get used to it, Ross. There's no privacy in this town. Everyone knows you guys dated before and that you left. Expect some glares and probably a few hard questions."

Great, more pressure. "I can handle a few glares." He checked himself over in the mirror above the dresser. He looked pretty good for a man his age. He'd be fifty-five next week. He had a bit more gray than last year, but was still fit and strong and damned proud of it. "Come on, guys, I need coffee, and I have just enough time before I pick her up."

What he really needed was a stiff drink to calm his nerves, but that wasn't happening. No way he'd show up to a date with alcohol on his breath. It dawned on him that today was basically their fourth date. First was the pub the day after they met. Second was the Winterfest Dance. Third was the night in the pub where Tom had ditched them.

He's seen Nora a few times between, but this was an actual date. Outside, with people. Not just television or fabulous sex.

He decided to start fresh. He'd bring her flowers. "Dec, text Cyn and find out what Nora's favorite flowers are, will ya?" He was surprised when Dec sent the text without ribbing him first.

"Chrysanthemums and daisies. Cyn says get Gerbera daisies because you won't find mums this time of year."

"Thanks."

Before he knew it, he was standing on Nora's front step, daisies and some tiny white flowers that looked like mini-carnations in hand. He rang the bell, and she instantly opened the door. His heart dropped to his toes and rebounded up. Holy shit! She was gorgeous. Her hair was styled in an elegant updo. Her dress clung to her curves like a lover. He wanted to strip her naked right there. He swallowed hard, clearing his nerves and banking his arousal. He would not sleep with her tonight. He'd decided that earlier. This was their first real date.

"Nora, you look incredible." He held out the flowers as he stepped inside, closing the outer door behind him.

She took them and opened the outer wrapping. "Oh, they're lovely. My favorites. Thank you. You've been researching," she teased.

"I confess to having Dec ask. I wanted them to be perfect." Great, now he was confessing his nerves. He wanted her to think he was smooth and charming, not a nervous dweeb.

"I appreciate your thoughtfulness. Not many men would take the time to care." She brushed a kiss across his cheek and sent his pulse skyrocketing. At this rate, she was going to give him a heart attack.

♥♥♥

Ross's hand was warm on her back as they followed the hostess through Tamarack to their table. She seated them and handed them each a sheet of cardstock with the menu printed on it.

"Today, your chef, Andre, has selected a prime rib dinner as the feature. There are a few other choices," she said.

152

Nora glanced at the few selections. Everything sounded delicious.

"Andre cooks what he wants," the hostess said. "He's temperamental, but I guarantee that whatever you order, it will be perfect and delicious. Your server will be right with you."

"It all looks incredible." Nora scanned the selections again.

"I think I'll do the prime rib and lobster special, though I doubt the lobster will be fresh."

"You'd be wrong on that," a tall thin man with broad shoulders stepped up to the table, "I keep a tank of live lobsters in the back. Nothing here is frozen." He offered his hand to Nora. "I'm Andre, your chef. Welcome to Tamarack."

"Nice to meet you. I'm Nora, this is Ross." She was startled that the chef showed up at their table even before they ordered. It didn't fit his temperamental reputation. They chatted for a few minutes, and he took their orders himself. Unusual but interesting.

She chatted with Ross about the plans for the gallery. He was worried that he'd let them all down.

"I'm a mathematician, not an art critic. What if I screw this up?"

"You won't. You just have to be personable with the artists and guests. Talk to them, show them around. Arrange purchases and shipping. You've got a mind for details, so you'll be great. In your spare time, you can do the books. We've got an accountant for the big stuff, but you can handle day to day details. With your math-based mind, you'll be great."

"I can't believe it's only a month to the gala grand opening. What will we serve? I've organized wines from a local vintner, but I have no idea on food."

"Well, if Andre is as good as they say he is, maybe we can hire him."

They dropped the subject and talked turned to things more personal. "How are you enjoying retirement?" she asked.

"I'm busier now than when I worked." He laughed. "Actually, I'm loving it. I've only been here for a month and I've already got new friends, a weekly poker game, and a job that I'm actually enjoying. I've met this lovely woman and I'm hoping to see her again, unless I mess up our first real date." His smile betrayed his nerves.

Dinner was incredible. The food was exquisite, the company even better. Ross was easy to talk to, and it was amazing to spend time with him outside of the bedroom. Not that she wanted to jump right back into bed with him.

Okay, she did, but she wasn't going to. They'd gone that route. Now, she wanted to get to know him first. Sex could come later. But not too much later.

Ross gave her a chaste kiss goodnight.

"Thank you for a lovely evening." He brushed a kiss across her cheek.

"Thank you. Would you like to come in for a glass of wine?" For the life of her, she didn't know if she wanted him to come in or to refuse.

"I'd like that, but I've got an early meeting at the gallery about some display units. Perhaps next time?"

His disappointment was clear in his voice. He meant the words, she could tell. "Next time," she promised and stepped inside.

They dated a couple times a week until June. Everything was lovely, but Ross still seemed reluctant to talk about the future. Nora was getting anxious. She was ready to make a commitment to Ross and hoped he felt the same. She was reluctant to push the issue because of the way it had busted them up at Christmas. She didn't want to rock the boat. So, she let it rest.

Now, she lay in bed, staring at the ceiling. Today, her two best friends had gotten married. The double ceremony had been touching and emotional. Standing at the front of the church, she'd watched Ross more than the brides and grooms. He looked—odd, maybe a bit nervous. She couldn't quite put her finger on what she read in his face. It wasn't like any of his usual moods, and she thought she'd learned them all.

He wasn't always great about sharing his feelings, but with a bit of prodding, he opened up to her. Because of this, she'd learned to read his moods. Right now, he looked like he was torn between being there for his brothers and cutting and running.

Was he scared? What could he be afraid of?

Before she could puzzle it out, the happy couples were off to get pictures taken and she and Ross were racing to the community center to be sure everything was on point for the reception.

Several exhausting hours later, she rolled over in bed and watched the even rise and fall of his chest as he slept. Her heart ached. She wanted to ask him what had been bothering him, and she wanted to know if he was starting to see a future with her. Soon, she was going to have to ask because for all that she loved him with every inch of her being, she needed to hear that he was committed to their relationship.

He rolled over and his eyes opened. "Hi, beautiful. Come here and kiss me."

God, she loved him so much.

Chapter Seventeen

Ross lay staring at the ceiling, listening to Nora sleep. She didn't snore exactly, just tiny puffs of air. It was sweet. He'd watched her for hours after she drifted off. God, she was an incredible woman. She scared him to death. He was terrified of her, of what he was feeling.

They'd made love twice last night. The second time was slow and sweet, and somehow very emotionally deep. He couldn't quite fathom what he felt, but it scared him to the depths of his soul.

His heart pounded every time he thought about her, and he felt this happy little glow surround him. It felt so much like what he'd felt for his wife, Martha, but it couldn't possibly be...love. He was afraid to even think the word.

He had fallen hard for Nora. He was in deep. She felt so right beside him, from the very second he set eyes on her, she'd felt like part of him.

He'd been with his brothers when Nora and her two friends came down the street. He'd barely noticed Eve and Cynthia, though his brothers sure had. Nora had stolen his entire attention and his breath.

Even now, months later, she had that power. He was torn between sheer terror of not seeing her again and of losing her.

Mathematically, it was nearly incalculable that he'd find a second soul mate after his wife and childhood sweetheart died. But with Nora, it felt like he had.

Math was never wrong. That meant his heart was leading him astray, trapping him into something unescapable. He wanted to bolt. Run as fast and as far as he could. Yet he wanted to stay, right here at her side.

He rolled toward her and pulled her into his arms. A soft smile graced her lips, and she rolled toward him, snuggling into his side with a soft smile. He could stay here, with Nora at his side…forever.

Panic swamped him.

No!

He wasn't ready for permanence. Not yet. He couldn't do this. He couldn't bear thinking about losing her the way he'd lost Martha. It would kill him.

"Dramatic much?" he grumbled to himself.

"What's wrong?" she asked, sleep making her voice husky and sexy.

"Nothing." He wouldn't admit to being terrified of losing her. It would unman him.

"You're fidgeting like you've got ants in your pants. Your heart is racing." She sat up and looked down at him with a puzzled frown. "What's wrong?"

"Nothing. I'm not good at sleeping in, I guess." He almost winced at the lie. He loved staying in bed late, drinking coffee, and reading. Or just snoozing off and on.

She glanced at the bedside clock. "It's only five. We barely went to bed." Her blush was adorable. He couldn't help but sit up and brush a kiss across her forehead.

"I'm good," he lied again. The words felt like daggers to his conscience.

"No, you're not. Something is bothering you. I'll make coffee." She pulled a blanket from the tangle of bedding and wrapped it around herself before scurrying into the bathroom.

He'd done that. He'd made her upset and self-conscious. Damn. He'd taken a lovely evening and ruined it. They'd had a wonderful time dancing at his brothers' dual wedding. He was a jackass. Guilt swamped him.

Between the guilt and the fear, he was overwhelmed. His chest got tight, and he gasped for air as he stared at the closed bathroom door. Behind it, Nora muttered something under her breath; water splashed and the cupboard door closed with a bang.

Jesus! He'd hurt her.

He had to get out of here, before he hurt her worse.

He snatched up his pants and struggled into them. Shirt in hand, he made sure he had his keys and wallet and got the hell out of there. As he thundered down the stairs toward the front door, she called after him to wait. He didn't even pause.

He was shivering in the early morning cold and halfway to Declan's house before he realized he'd left behind his jacket and his shoes. Fudge on toast.

"I'm an asshole and a total screw-up."

He crept into the house, grabbed his laptop, and threw on some clothing. Before anyone could notice he was home, he was back on the road, headed toward the airport. He had no idea where he was going, just as long as it was far from Nora. He needed distance to get his shit together. He could almost hear his brothers' recriminations and picture the disapproval on his mother's face. If she was alive, she'd kick his ass around the block and back again.

His hands trembled and his knees shook.

Just outside of town, he found a side road and pulled off the highway. He put his car into park and sat there, shaking and berating himself for being a chickenshit. Mad at himself, he punched the roof of the car. Pain radiated up his arm.

Good, he deserved to hurt after what he'd just done. He should be tarred and feathered. Or sent to a place where math had no rules or made no sense. He was the worst type of despicable.

Their Christmas Love

Chapter Eighteen

Nora glared down the stairs. Ross had slammed the front door in his haste to leave. "What the hell?" He'd probably woken Melissa.

Straightening her spine, she went back into her bedroom and pulled on some ratty sweats and a long-sleeved T-shirt. "Now what?"

Somewhere, between the time she fell asleep after making love the second time and when his restless movements had woken her, her relationship with Ross had gone dramatically wrong. She replayed the night over in her head. He'd been a careful and attentive lover, and she'd done her best to give more than she took. They'd had fun. Well, she'd had more than fun and thought he had as well...unless he faked two orgasms, and she couldn't imagine him doing that.

Of course, she couldn't imagine him bolting from her bedroom like his ass was on fire and she had a bucket

165

of gas either. The least he could have done was say goodbye. She stomped down the stairs for coffee.

She walked upstairs, stepped into the studio, closed the door and leaned against it. The shades were drawn; she was in total darkness. Like her heart. She slid her back down the door until she was crouched in a little ball. Her coffee thudded on the vinyl plank flooring beside her. It made a small slosh. She didn't care that she'd spilled.

She'd suspected what she felt for Ross was stronger than he felt. If he wasn't ready for a commitment, he could have just said so. Men were jerks. How was it that the first time she'd really opened herself up to a man after her ugly divorce, he bolted? Twice.

What kind of man did that? Who slept with a woman, in both senses of the word, and took off, half naked when she woke up? She was no sex siren, but it couldn't have been that bad. She'd believed they shared a connection. Had she been wrong?

Wait. He'd been weird at the wedding. Nervous or something.

It hit her like a ton of bricks.

He wasn't ready to commit. Waking beside her had spooked him, and he'd taken off. Freaking cowardly jerk.

She wrapped her arms around her knees and rocked back and forth. Tears welled in her eyes, and she refused to let them fall. He didn't deserve that power over her. She'd thought they connected over the past few months. They'd talked about their dreams and hinted at a future together. She wasn't alone in that conversation, that was for damn sure. He'd been right there alongside of her all the way. In the sex and in the conversation.

"Crap on toast." She stood and grabbed her mug. She wiped up the spill with her sock and flipped on the Christmas lights that ran around the ceiling of her studio. She wasn't ready to face full light. "Asshat. Jerk. Weiner."

She pulled out a large canvas. Four feet square, it might be big enough to hold her rage. She propped it on a low easel, grabbed her black spray paint, and covered every inch of the surface. While the paint dried, she chugged her coffee and got another one. Luckily, she was alone for the day. She wasn't fit company. Nor would she be until she came to grips with the tangled ball of snakes that were her emotions.

"Stupid man," she muttered around the biscotti she held between her teeth. Another biscotti and coffee in hand, she stomped upstairs.

Right now, all she cared about was getting her hurt and rage out of her system. Bottled up emotion could kill a woman. She'd even read that unaddressed emotions could cause cancer. She wasn't sure she believed that, but she wasn't taking any chances either.

A quick touch revealed that the spray paint was dry enough to work with, though it was still tacky. She eyed up her oil paints and her acrylics. Arms crossed over her chest, she stared into her metal-doored paint cabinet. Nothing sparked interest.

Wait! She had some old spray paint in the garage. It wasn't her usual medium, but it could work. She was to the garage and back with paint and a chunk of cardboard in minutes. She'd hoped for more colors, but yellow, red, orange, purple, and silver would have to do.

She draped some old sheets on everything in the room, including the floor. This could be messy. She set the cardboard on another easel and experimented with different distances and burst lengths to see what she could achieve. It was hard to find what she needed, but after a few minutes and more than a little paint, she had a workable technique. She should have paid more attention to those street artists last summer. She'd watched them with idle curiosity rather than with an eye for learning the technique. Mistake. She knew better.

Red paint in hand, she approached the black canvas. She froze there, unsure what came next. She wasn't often at a loss in the creative process. Right now, she felt constricted. Like her muse was tied up in the closet, or gone on vacation. Or dead.

No! She wasn't going to let him steal her art again. She'd recovered last time and wasn't going to let him ruin her now. Nothing would kill her creative drive.

Defiantly, she approached the canvas. A spot of red here, a slash there. A swipe of yellow that tapered off to nothing. Another. Some orange down the center. She spritzed and stroked. A few lines of purple.

Slowly, the ragged form of a bonfire emerged. She swallowed hard and dropped to her knees when she realized the purple and silver formed a Picasso-like man standing in the fire. Definitely in, not behind.

She dropped the silver can; it rolled away and thumped with finality against the door as her tears began to fall. She curled into a ball on the floor and let the pain wash over her. She thought she knew him, and his betrayal cut as deeply as when Dickhead had cheated and dumped her.

She could handle a lie, or even cheating, but this betrayal, the abandonment was more than her heart could take. She wept until she couldn't cry anymore. And then, she wept again.

She awoke to night's darkness, unsure how long she'd slept. Eyes closed, she ran through a couple stretches, working up the courage to face last night's work.

She pivoted around, eyes closed. Steeling herself, she peeked one eye open. Yikes! She stared at the image. It was darker than anything she'd done. She saw her rage there, in the fire, the dark background, the burning man. Somehow amid the conflagration, she'd painted a heart dripping blood.

"Man, do I have issues." She laughed wryly. "Not my usual work, but it does evoke an emotion." She'd like to hide it away, but the surface was tacky, especially where layer after layer had landed. Nothing to do but let it dry. She picked up the tea and yesterday's coffee mug, flicked off the Christmas lights, and fled downstairs. Her phone chimed.

Ross.

Not happening. She deleted the message without reading it and turned off her ringer. Cyn and Eve were on their honeymoons. She was alone until Melissa got home from her father's.

The screen lit up a few times during the movie, and again during the next one. Resolutely, she resisted the urge to peek. She had no time for Ross's crap. When her conscience told her he might be apologizing, and that she should hear him out, she told it to shut up.

Their Christmas Love

Chapter Nineteen

Ross climbed into the small airplane on his way home from a trip to check out a couple other galleries for ideas on displays for their gallery. When the trip was booked, he'd been optimistic that he'd finally have made up with Nora. He was going to ask her to travel with him. Instead, he'd turned chicken and ran away.

Fat chance.

She hated him and was ignoring him.

God, his heart ached. He'd been an idiot and had panicked and bolted. It was a total jack-hole move. He'd raced out of town like his ass was on fire. He'd only gone fifty miles when he turned around and came home.

He'd tried calling and texting Nora to apologize. She'd ignored every attempt. He didn't blame her one bit. But her refusal to talk to him was going on months. She never came into the gallery when he was there. If he came in while she was working, he left immediately. He'd hoped for some softening by the time this trip arose. How could he explain the mess his emotions and thoughts were if she didn't open up to him?

All he wanted was ten minutes. In person. On the phone. Via video chat. Anything. Her friends had flat-out refused to help him. He appreciated their loyalty, but couldn't they cut him some slack here? His brothers were even less helpful, if that was even possible.

He missed her. His stomach ached. He'd lost weight. He'd stopped going to the gym. He needed a haircut but didn't go because his stylist's hair was the same color as Nora's. Pathetic.

Summer came and went. Then fall. November was cold and snowy. It was hard to believe he'd known Nora for a full year and couldn't get close to her. He was the worst kind of jackass.

He was barely surviving. He ate enough to keep alive. He watched sappy romances and asked his brothers endless questions about Nora which they refused to answer. His life sucked. He never should have left Florida.

Chapter Twenty

There was nobody but him, the pilot, and the pilot's wife on the charter to Valley Springs. Not that he'd expected anything else. The airport there was tiny, you could land a small plane like this, or a helicopter, but nothing larger. He settled into his seat of the Textron Aviation Beechcraft Bonanza G36. This was the Cadillac of small six seaters.

He pulled out his tablet and started reviewing the airplanes specs. He loved anything that flew. The flight would be about an hour and a half, takeoff to landing, so he had plenty of time for reading, and reading was better than beating himself up for screwing up with Nora.

It seemed like they'd only taken off when the pilot advised him to buckle up for a rough landing. It was snowing heavily in Valley Springs. His stomach pitched at the rough touchdown, but he held it together. He used to fly a lot for NASA, and he had endured much worse.

"Are you okay here?" the pilot shouted over the wind. "We've got to get going before the worst of the storm arrives."

"Go. I'll be fine. I've got a ride coming. Thanks for the flight." The words were barely out of his mouth when the engines' whine told him they were leaving. Fast.

He scurried to the shelter of a nearby hangar, snow and ice crystals battered about by the engines pounded into his face. Close to the building, his turned his back to the plane. In seconds, he was alone in the near silence. The wind gusted, snow flew around him, but without the force of the engines to push it, the weather was almost tolerable, just darned cold. Cold and painful, like his heart.

He pulled his thick jacket from his duffle bag, slipped it on, and texted Dec to let him know he'd arrived. No answer. "He must be on his way." The small airport was a mile and a half outside of town. Too far to walk in this weather, at least when you were dragging a suitcase and laptop. He stared at the heavy black bag at his feet, wishing it had wheels. He'd stuffed the duffle with clothing and the Christmas gifts he'd bought his brothers and their new wives.

He tucked the bag close to the hangar and wandered around its perimeter. There were no doorways or alcoves. He jogged to the next hangar. No hiding spots there either. Damn. He snuggled deeper into his jacket and hunched his shoulders. If he stood just right, he could protect his face from the worst of the wind.

He waited. And waited. He shot off another text. The temperature was dropping rapidly. At some point, he was going to have to abandon his bags and start walking. Maybe he'd catch a ride from a passing vehicle. Yeah, if they didn't hit him by mistake. Walking to town in a near blizzard probably wasn't the best idea.

He should have worn boots. But who wore boots on a plane? He'd thought runners a better choice for the flight. His aching, frozen toes were disagreeing with that decision. At least he'd stuffed his jacket and gloves in his duffle. That would stave off hypothermia for a while.

Once upon a time, he'd loved winter. Florida had made him soft. He sighed.

He was as soft as Nora's skin. Standing in the freezing wind, he could almost smell her unique scent. Not a perfume, but scented soap and floral shampoo. He'd nearly lost his mind in a crowded elevator at his last hotel. He'd been squished in beside a woman with the same shampoo scent. He'd been miserable for the rest of the day.

Perhaps he'd see her this week. Maybe if she was desperate, and he was lucky, he'd even get to talk to her. He couldn't wait to see her smile. More likely her frown, but he'd take what he could get.

He'd been an idiot and a jerk after the wedding. He'd panicked and ran. He'd pictured himself growing old, older, with her. His entire world would change. He'd been single most of his life, since Martha died. He kept thinking about being close to Nora, risking losing her too. The very idea terrified him.

He'd thought he couldn't risk losing her, so he'd bolted.

He was a total idiot. He'd lost her anyway, and now he couldn't get her back. All his life he'd made decisions quickly, without dithering over them. Unfortunately, he'd panicked and abandoned her. He would understand if she kept up the cold shoulder routine. He couldn't blame her. He hadn't even said goodbye. The more time that passed, the harder it was going to be to fix his screw-up.

Remorse hung on his shoulders like a lead cape. His chest went tight, and he tried to massage away the ache. He could see her face in his mind. The ache got worse.

Toot! Toot!

The car horn startled him. He hadn't heard the vehicle arrive though the raging wind. He spun around, snatched up his bags, and sprinted from behind the building. Declan's truck was nowhere in sight. Neither was Tom's pickup. A little red Jeep YJ sat at the edge of the tarmac. It might not be his family, but he'd beg for a ride if he had to. Face down, he scurried forward.

He popped open the back door and threw in his bags. He climbed in front and closed the door. He turned to his savior. Angry blue eyes glared at him from under a bright floral ear band. "Nora. Thanks for coming." He had a million questions, a thousand apologies, and a least a hundred hours of groveling to do, and he could barely formulate a greeting.

179

He wasn't even buckled in when the Jeep lurched forward with a spin off its tires. Yeah, he was in deep crap and he deserved it.

"Thank you for coming," he repeated. "I wouldn't have blamed you if you left me to freeze to death."

She slammed on the brakes and fishtailed to a stop. "Do you really think so little of me that you believe I'd let someone freeze to death? I wouldn't do that to my worst enemy, though I was tempted. Trust me, I debated leaving you to freeze your worthless nuts off." Her teeth ground together audibly.

"I'm sorry." *Pathetic answer, idiot. You're supposed to be impressing her or begging for forgiveness.*

"Oh, you're sorry?" Sarcasm rang from her voice. "And what exactly are you sorry for? Leading me on, thinking we could build something together? For screwing me and taking off in the middle of the night? For abandoning me without a goodbye? For pestering me with calls and texts and damned emails? Or how about for thinking I'd leave you outside to freeze to death? Pick one. You've got a lot to apologize for, mister, and I'm not feeling the least bit forgiving." She put the Jeep in gear and started forward.

"I'm sorry for all of it. I screwed up."

She slammed on the brakes, and they swung sideways, narrowly missing the ditch. "Screwed up? Screwed up?" Her voice was shrill with disbelief. He thought she muttered "idiot" under her breath, but he couldn't be certain. She twisted the wheel and stepped on the gas.

"Nora, I apologize for being an idiot. I woke beside you and saw my future pass before my eyes. My entire life. I could easily see a life with you. But what if you died, like my first wife? I'd be alone. It would kill me. It freaked me out."

She braked again. Her hands were white knuckled on the steering wheel. She shifted into neutral, pulled the emergency brake, and unbuckled her seatbelt. Her teeth clicked together and she spun to face him.

"Did I ask you to give up anything? Did I ever hint that I wanted you to?" She shook her head and glared. Her eyes shone with tears. She blinked them away.

"No—"

She cut him off before he could finish his response. He hated himself for thinking it, but angry Nora was as sexy as hell.

"Listen to me, Mr. NASA Mathematician. You aren't all that. Not one bit. I can't believe that you think that you're so freaking fantastic that I'd try and force you into a long-term relationship. You're certifiable."

"I thought we had a relationship?"

"Oh, you infuriate me. Let me put you straight. I went out with you and slept with you because I liked you. I like sex. Having a man around is nice. I never asked you to change your life and I never will. Pull your head out of your arse and get a grip on that ego. You're not as great as you think you are."

She buckled up and pulled onto the highway.

"I'd like to talk about it," he pleaded.

"And I'd like you to shut up."

Chapter Twenty-One

Nora stifled a groan and started cleaning up her painting mess. Had she really told Ross to shut up? She was the one that was certifiable. She was never that rude, not even when she was in the complete control of her muse and ignoring everyone and everything. She paced her studio. Three days had passed since she'd driven him home from the airport.

She banked her disgust. She'd liked Ross, but it was obvious that he wasn't ready to advance their relationship beyond something casual. With a sigh, she washed her brushes and went downstairs.

She couldn't even ask her friends for help. Declan and Cyn were gone to Hawaii for two weeks. Eve and Tom were on an Alaskan cruise. Having both friends on their second honeymoon in the first year sucked. It was even worse. Dickhead had taken Melissa to Disneyland for Christmas.

It was Christmas Eve, and she was alone. She'd never been alone for the holidays. Not once in her entire life.

Downstairs, she piled ice cream into a bowl, lit a fire, and flopped in front of the television. Maybe a good cry from a romantic movie would help cheer her up.

Why did Ross's betrayal hurt so bad? She shoveled a scoop of ice cream into her mouth and grabbed the remote to flip through the channels.

Channel after channel was showing holiday specials. Cooking, Christmas baking, holiday rom-coms. She finally settled on *Mistletoe and Molly*, a romance by Canadian author Jennifer Snow. She'd seen it a dozen times since its release, and it never failed to cheer her up.

By the final kiss, she was crying like a baby. The movie had given her an epiphany. She needed Ross in her life. She loved him more than she'd ever loved anyone else. Christmas was about love and forgiveness. Maybe she could get beyond Ross's betrayal and forgive him, because God knows she wasn't able to forget about him.

She'd ragged on him about being immature and unable to commit. But was she really any better, any more mature? She was being a total witch.

She sat there as the end credits rolled and the ads began, thinking about the past year. She'd met him just over fourteen months ago. She'd lost her heart to him instantly. If she were honest with herself, she'd admit that she'd rushed him; that's why he'd bolted the first time.

She'd been lucky he came back and that they'd been able to get beyond that fight. Had she pushed him again? She replayed the wedding and the evening that followed.

No. This time it wasn't her. This was all on him. He'd gotten scared, he'd said so in the car, and she'd told him to shut up. She was as stubborn as he was.

She ate a few chocolates from the open box on the coffee then chided herself for eating her emotions. Sadness crept in. She'd screwed this up as badly as he had. Maybe there was a way to change things.

"If I can't have him forever, maybe I can have him for a while." She crossed her arms and glared at the television as it started another holiday romance. "I still love him; I probably always will. I'm sure he cares. I just have to convince him. But how?"

She wished her friends were here. They'd have some good ideas.

Ross stared at the television. He'd binge watched twenty-four hours of holiday specials straight. Every single one of them carried the same messages: Be kind, be generous, admit your faults, love your friends. If you could do that, life would turn out fine.

Hypothetical nonsense.

Except that it rang true in his heart.

He'd watched a romantic flick about a woman who'd lost her husband and had gone on a whirlwind tour of the world and found love again.

He'd found a second love too. Only he'd messed it up. He had to find a way to fix it because as scared as he was of something bad happening to Nora, he was pathetic without her. He needed her. His need was greater than his fear.

As he watched yet another movie that made his eyes well with happy tears, he got an idea. He shot a text off to Tom.

♥♥♥

Nora's phone chimed with a message.

Eve: Can you go to the town office and pick up an envelope for me? Apparently, they need it gone right away, before they close for Christmas.

Nora checked her watch. It was three-fifteen on Christmas Eve and the office would close early. If she hurried, she could just make it.

Nora: Sure. On my way in five.

Eve: Thanks.

She tied her hair and put on clean, non-paint-splattered clothing and headed out. She had time to walk, and the exercise would do her good after so long on the couch. She bundled up against the cold and locked up the house.

Every house was lit with holiday lights. Inflatable Santas waved gaily as she passed. Reindeer perched on rooftops. Frosty frolicked on every third lawn. Despite her deep hurt, she couldn't help but smile. Christmas had always been one of her favorite times of year.

The love, the giving, the forgiveness. Peace and joy. Every bit of it, religious and secular, spoke to her heart. Sure, she could skip the commercialism, but the rest of it was heaven, and a balm to her aching heart.

She passed through the school yard, trying not to remember being there with Ross last winter. She heard carolers singing in the town square and detoured to listen to them. The stood at the base of the town's enormous Christmas tree, singing song after song.

As she watched and listened, the song morphed into *I'll be Home for Christmas*, and the singers started walking slowly across the square. She followed their movements until her gaze landed on the small gazebo at the center of the square.

It glowed under the light from a thousand white fairy lights. A man knelt there; his head bowed low. He looked like he was praying, but that didn't stop the choir from surrounding the gazebo.

One of the singers, a friend of Cyn's from the library, waved Nora forward with a smile.

Weird.

Nora walked toward her. As she got close, the woman, she couldn't remember her name, waved her toward the man in the gazebo. "Go on then," she said. "He's waiting."

"What?"

"Just go. This is the season of love and forgiveness. Give him a chance."

She turned back to the gazebo. Ross slowly rose to his feet, a nervous expression on his face. He stepped left and bent to pick something up. He smiled at her.

Her heart skittered crazily.

Why was he here?

"Nora. Can I have two minutes of your time?" He held out an enormous bouquet of roses. "I couldn't get mums," he confessed. "I did try. It was either roses or lilies, and they make me think of funeral arrangements."

She thought she heard him mumble a curse under his breath.

"Wait. Give me a second. I'm nervous." He cleared his throat and straightened his tie, and she realized that he was wearing a suit, complete with dress shoes, and no jacket. He had to be freezing.

"How did you know I'd be here?" she asked the first question to coalesce into coherent words.

"I sent for you. The text was a ruse. I didn't know what else to do."

She braced herself to keep from rushing into his arms and begging him to keep her in his life. He seemed bent on doing something, and she didn't want to interrupt for her own needs.

"I sent for you because I need to talk to you."

The choir morphed into a quiet version of *Last Christmas*.

"I'm listening," she barely got the words past the lump in her throat. She stepped onto the first step of the gazebo and took the flowers in one hand. He offered a hand and helped her into the gazebo, under the roof, out of the drifting snow. Snow would always remind her of Ross.

He cleared his throat again and stared at his shoes for ten full seconds. "I messed up. I got scared. I woke up in your bed and knew I wanted to spend the rest of my life there."

"And that's a bad thing?" she asked without meaning to interrupt him.

"Yes. No. Wait. At the time, it seemed horrible. I've been married before. When Martha died, I nearly did too. Watching you sleep, I was struck by a totally irrational fear that you'd die too and I'd be left alone."

She didn't speak, sensing he had more to say.

"I was a fool. I lost you more completely by running than if you had passed. I totally miscalculated."

She loved the math speak.

"My math was off. Way off. I bolted and then I recalculated. You wouldn't hear me out, and I don't blame you. The odds of you forgiving me were astronomical."

She was starting to warm up to his method of apology. The choir fell silent, but didn't move away.

"I love you, Nora Ravine, more than life itself. I'd give up everything for you, including my pride. So, I tricked you into coming here. I knew I needed a grand gesture. This is it. My heart, on a plate, for you. In public. I want to spend the rest of my life with you. I'm incomplete without you in my world. Please forgive me."

He dropped to one knee and dug in his pocket. He pulled out a black velvet box, opened it, and thrust it toward her. A glittering red, heart-shaped stone stared up at her.

"Here it is, my heart, for you. Will you forgive me, will you marry me and let me be a stepfather to your wonderful daughter? Will you be my wife and grow old, older, at my side?" His voice trembled. "Please?"

"You mean it? Forever? With me?"

"Yes. With you and Melissa. Here, there, anywhere you want to go. I'll follow and be your supporter, your slave. Anything, just take me back into your life."

She pretended to consider his question, though her heart was thundering in her ears. Her whole body felt like it was soaring into heaven. Bliss settled on her shoulders and a certainty that life with Ross was what she needed.

"Okay, I guess." She winked. "Yes, Ross, I will marry you. Forever."

The choir cheered and broke into a chorus of *Halleluiah.*

She laughed. Ross laughed.

He jumped to his feet, yanked her into his arms, and stole her breath with an earth-shaking, heart-moving, love-filled kiss.

If you enjoyed this story, please check out my other Christmas books.
A Melody for Christmas
Coming Home for Christmas
Sleigh Bells Inn
Christmas in Silver Creek.

Their Christmas Love

About Katie O'Connor

Best-selling author Katie O'Connor lives in Calgary, Alberta, Canada. She married her high school sweetheart and is living her happily ever after. She is the mother of two grown daughters and is extremely proud of her five grandchildren.

She is the founder of The Write Chicks, a private romance writers' group set up with the sole purpose of supporting each other's writing career. She belongs to several other writing organizations.

Katie's career path has been long and twisted, with most of her life devoted to her family. She's been a waitress, chambermaid, cashier, store manager, as well as a lab and X-ray technician. She's been a small business owner and is an avid quilter and crafter.

She's dabbled in writing since high school because something drives her to create stories. She swears it's impossible for her NOT to write. Unsatisfied with one genre, Katie writes contemporary romance, erotic romance, fantasy/paranormal romance, romantic suspense, and erotica.

Katie believes in all things magical, including dragons, fairies, UFOs, ghosts, and house pixies. But most of all she believes in love, romance, and hope.

Where to Find Katie

One of Katie's favorite things is hearing from her readers. If you enjoyed this book, don't hesitate to reach out and let Katie knows.

Email: katie@katieohwrites.com
Newsletter Signup: http://eepurl.com/Q2nRr
Website: https://katieohwrites.com
Facebook: http://www.facebook.com/katieohwrites

Katie's Books

Contemporary Romance by Katie

Heart's Haven
Running Home
Saving Grace
Building Trust

Coyote Creek
A Lesson in Love
A Heart Torn Apart
A Secret to Shatter
A Melody for Christmas
A Surrender so Sweet
A Place Called Home
A Love to Rebuild
Coming Home for Christmas

A Silver Fox Christmas
Their Perfect Christmas
Their Christmas Heart
Their Christmas Love

<u>Contemporary Romance Single Title</u>
To a Tea
Rekindled Fire
Hearts in the Spotlight (A Women of Stampede Novel)
Cupid's Charm
Gingerbread Dreams
Christmas in Silver Creek
Sleigh Bells Inn (A Christmas at the Inn Novella) (Dec. 2022)

<u>Romantic Suspense</u>
Protecting Josie
Bulletproof Heart

<u>Paranormal Romance</u>
Fire Magic (Three Moon Falls Book One)
Water Magic (Three Moon Falls Book Two)

<u>Career Planning</u>
Creative Career Planning Workbook for Authors

<u>Erotic Romance/Erotica</u>

<u>Stand Alone Erotic Romances</u>
Tessa's Trio
The Gift
<u>Covet the Cowboy Erotic Romance Series</u>
Corralling the Cowboy (Book 1)
Cornering the Cowgirl (Book 2)

Katie O'Connor